SNOWED IN WITH MY *Pucking* EX

WALL STREET JOURNAL & USA TODAY BESTSELLING AUTHOR

SAPPHIRE KNIGHT

SNOWED IN WITH MY PUCKING EX

By Sapphire Knight

Wall Street Journal & USA Today Bestselling Author

COPYRIGHT 2025 SAPPHIRE KNIGHT

ALL RIGHTS RESERVED

Editing by Sapphire Knight

Formatting by Sapphire Knight

Cover Design by Sapphire Knight

This book is a work of fiction. Any references to real events, real people, and real places are used fictitiously. Other names, characters, places, and incidents are products of the author's imagination, and any resemblance to persons, living or dead, actual events, organizations, or places is entirely coincidental.

All rights are reserved. This book is intended for the purchaser of this book ONLY. No part of this book may be reproduced or transmitted in any form or by any means, graphic, electronic, or mechanical, including photocopying, recording, taping, or by any information storage retrieval system, without the express written permission of the author. All songs, song titles, and lyrics contained in this book are the property of the respective songwriters and copyright holders. All AI use is PROHIBITED.

BLURB

It was the holidays in Noel Falls, and nothing was quicker to bring me home than Christmastime surrounded by my family. I'd jumped in my little car, happily singing carols, way too noisily, and sipped hot cocoa the entire way. I was off work and ready to spend my vacation the right way, with a stomach full of freshly baked cookies and time spent with my best friend.

Imagine my surprise when the first man I run into isn't a hunky lumberjack, but my superstar hockey player ex-boyfriend. He's the one I've always deemed got away, who's had me comparing every man I've met to him. Of course, fate would place him in my path when I least expect it, but that doesn't mean I have to give in, right?

With the holiday festival quickly coming up, and my family counting on me, the pressure stacks up. From one obstacle to another, I'm left in a coffee shop contemplating what to do next. One thing I'm certain of is that I don't need the help of a do-gooder ex-boyfriend showing up to save the day. Too bad he has plans of his own to win me back, and when we're accidentally snowed in at my family's cabin…

Fighting fate is harder than I ever imagined.

SAPPHIRE KNIGHT

TROPES

-Independent but caring MFC

-Golden retriever MMC

-Snowed in

-One bed

-Professional hockey player

-Happily ever after

-Second chance

-He falls first

-Friends to lovers

-Sweet with a little spice

-Holiday festivities

-Acts of service and love

-Small town contemporary romance

About the cast:

A grandma with no filter, a mom obsessed with mistletoe, a grumpy grandpa, a father who is devoted to his family, a gossiping best friend with a couple of wild kids, a group of nosey hockey players who are all experts in dating (or so they believe), and of course, the townsfolk... who are Christmas crazy, and all about being in everyone's business!

Dedicated To:

You, the person who makes the season magical.

Women don't get enough credit for making the season as whimsical and memorable as we do. Without us, Christmas would probably suck, so buy yourself that paperback or special coffee you want. *You deserve it.*

SAPPHIRE KNIGHT

DEAR READER:

Hi! If you're a seasoned reader of mine, you'll be expecting grit, lots of spice, plot twists coming out of nowhere, and triggers. I want to let you know, this is nothing like my other books. I got presented with the challenge of, "Can you write a Hallmark, cutsey style romance book for the holidays?" By my family. Of course, I said yes! I've been wanting to dive into hockey romance and thought this would be the perfect occasion.

I started writing, and instead of a quick, fluffy romance to share for Christmas, the words kept coming and coming. The next thing I knew, this was turning out to be my longest book all year! I did go back and add some more spice and tension between the two main leads as I was reading through it, but I hope you will enjoy the plot for what it is truly meant to be.

A sweet romance that's sprinkled with a touch of spice, to celebrate finding love when you least expect it. And, learning to not only embrace the holiday craziness no matter what life throws at you, but also to accept help when it's needed.

I hope you have a very Merry Christmas and that this season is magical for you, filled with love and friendship. Thank you for reading this. You're making my real-life dreams come true by picking up this book.

XO- Sapph

SAPPHIRE KNIGHT

CHAPTER ONE

WINTER

"Fa-la-la-la-laaaaaa," I sing the carol loudly as I take in the snowy white winter wonderland before me. It must've just finished snowing this morning because the roads have been clear for the most part, and the fields remind me of pillowy blankets, undisturbed. When I received the call to come home for Christmas, I knew I had to oblige. Although it's not quite Christmas yet. It's not even Thanksgiving, but that's beside the point because we all know Christmas is a season, not just a date.

My gaze pings around the freshly swept snow that's piled on each side of the road, taking in the various snow drifts. It looks like I've stepped right into a postcard; it's so serene and beautiful. It's like I'm seeing it all for the first time, when in reality, I was lucky enough to grow up with this every year. Now, I can easily see that I'd taken advantage of it back then, ignoring nature's beauty for what it truly is. *Peace.*

Gah, I missed this place.

I know a large portion of people dread going home for the holidays, or simply returning to the town they grew up in-in general, but I'm not one of them. Especially not during the holidays. It's quite the opposite, in fact, and when I get the rare opportunity to return for Christmas, I can't seem to get back home fast enough.

I carefully remove the Styrofoam disposable cup from my center console cup holder and take a small sip. Even almost an hour later, the liquid is still hot. Like magic. Everything during this time of the year is a blissful wonder; the air is filled with crisp, freshly fallen snow, hot apple cider, or hot cocoa, people are a pleasant mix of cheerfulness, and kindness is spread in abundance. Don't get me started on the decorations. They're one of my favorite parts of all. The twinkling lights bring a touch of sparkle to even the simplest of items. Such as an old broken-down tractor in the middle of a pasture, and suddenly it's not a rusted piece of metal, but a feature piece, bringing the *"oh's and ah's"* from a person driving by.

"Per-rum-pum-pum-pummm," My voice fills the car as the next song plays. Another one of my favorites, but really, who doesn't have several favorite Christmas songs? I'd almost be worried if someone didn't have at least three they could belt out at a moment's notice.

Am I a little too cheery? Perhaps. However, I have good reason to be smiling from ear to ear. I've been blessed with the next month off from work, and I'm refusing to spoil even a single minute of it. I can't exactly afford that much time off in one big chunk, but that's where home comes in. I'll have a warm bed. The best cooking aside from my Nan's, God rest her soul. And, to top it off, I'll be able to work part-time at the holiday festival while I'm in town to help substitute for my normal income.

See? You'd be singing too.

Manheim Steamroller begins to play next as my little car scoots right along, my head bopping, hands moving like I'm heading up a symphony. I doubt that's the correct terminology for the guy who stands up at the front, flailing his hands around, but you get the picture. "This is what I'm talking about! Keep playing the good stuff, *Pandora*!" The only thing that'd make this any better right now is if Delilah were dj'ing, but they save her good stuff for later in the day.

"A composer!" I shout suddenly as the name comes to me. I'm glad there's no traffic around or they'd probably think I'm a crazy person right now, but I promise I'm not.

I can't help but beam as I think about what's to come. I'm one day closer to my mom's famous pumpkin pie, turkey dinner, and stuffing my gullet with all the rolls I can squirrel away. We'll watch football and eat way too much while Dad yells at whichever teams are playing in the big game. He'll probably complain as he does every year about there not being a hockey game on to watch afterward, but overall, he'll be in a good mood and try to help out wherever he can.

After Thanksgiving, cue all the Christmas shin-digs I love. There's the holiday renaissance fair in the next town over, the day after Thanksgiving, where they dress up in sweeping dresses and have a positively whimsical Mr. and Mrs. Claus taking pictures with everyone. Next comes our local holiday market, which is literally my favorite and the one I help work at each year. A week later, there is the children's Nutcracker performance at the theatre in the closest city, Noelville. After that, there's the local holiday dance held downtown, otherwise known as the Jingle Bell Swing, put on right before Christmas.

In between all of those fun activities, we fill in the twelve days until Christmas with our Advent calendars, which are full of candies and cheerful festive notes. We paint ornaments, trim the tree, and decorate the front porch. Then, we bake until my arms feel like they may fall off, and I need to be rolled out of the kitchen from consuming so many cookies. And, once all the baking is complete, we surprise friends, family, and neighbors with cookie baskets, along with holiday cards.

I think my number one favorite out of it all is when we watch a million *Hallmarky-type* movies in between all of the different events. Toss in some hockey and football games with Dad and Pop to keep things interesting. And then finally, last but one-hundred percent not least, spending Christmas day with the people I love the most while enjoying being *present*. It's a lot to take in, but I wouldn't have it any other way.

I pass the *'Welcome to the village of Noel Falls (Population 6,949)'* sign, and I can almost see home already. Not really, I'm actually almost at the bottom of a giant mountain I have to drive over first, but in my mind, I'm already picturing the long driveway leading to my family home. I carefully sip from my hot cocoa once more, humming in delight as the velvety, rich texture of sweet chocolate with whipped cream bursts over my tongue. I generally prefer mini marshmallows with sprinkles, and enough so that they fall out of the top of my mug, but they didn't have any. I figure beggars can't be choosers, though, and when I stopped to get gas, I saw they had my favorite cold-weather drink. Once I realized they also had vanilla cappuccino and that I could mix the two, I knew I had to have it. People who haven't mixed hot cocoa and vanilla cappuccino are surely missing out. I could live off the stuff if I didn't need to randomly supply my belly with tacos, pizza, and all the other fine fixin's out there.

I'm a foodie, in case you haven't figured that much already. It's one of the many things I struggle with, as I generally tend to want to overeat a little too much if I don't put my foot down and stop it. Needless to say, I have a butt. It's a big one, and some pretty banging curves if I do say so myself. I once heard the term more cushion for the pushin' and since then, I've decided I'm fine with my glorious love handles.

"Santa, baby, bring me a," I sing just as my car lets out a very unbecoming sputtering noise.

"Uh, did I just hear that correctly?" I glance at the speedometer, along with every other light and little symbol the screen on my car possesses, but it's not giving me any clues. The noise happens again, and my car drops speed for a moment before picking back up.

"What is that?" I continue talking to myself, hoping it'll give me a sign of some sort, which is pretty normal for me. Just then, it happens again, for a third time. Before I have a chance to further investigate, my brakes lock up and then my car begins to spin.

"Shoot, shoot, shoot!"

I turn into the slide and take my feet off the brake, hoping I'll eventually slow down, and this doesn't end up in a similar fashion as winter of twenty-eighteen did. Back then, I'd ended up sliding all over the road and had eventually plowed straight into a fence. My bad luck didn't end there, though, as I managed to keep sliding until my car was stuck in the middle of a giant cow pasture, somehow missing the bumper. It wasn't a good look, and it was a pain in the butt helping put the fence back together because that's what you do here. You see someone in need, or you mess up somehow, you pitch in to help fix whatever catastrophe there is. I'd had blisters on both hands for forever, it seemed, from learning how to put up a fence in the middle of winter.

My body shudders with the memory.

I'm steadily turning my wheel, attempting to keep a calm mind when the car begins to slide off to the side. No matter how many times I chant or do everything right, it slips off the road and right into the deeply piled snow. The same white stuff I'd been admiring and singing the praises of before. "You weren't sputtering, were you? You were hitting ice, and I wasn't paying close enough attention when it first happened." I sigh for the millionth time, running my hands over my face. "Rookie mistake, and I know better," I mutter dejectedly, shaking my head. I inhale deeply and then blow out a long breath, searching for my inner Zen.

I don't bother grabbing my cell, it'd only be a waste of time as I already know there's no reception right here. Having grown up in the area, I'm aware of all the spots where cell phone service is blocked; it's part of the curse of being in the mountains. Noel Falls happens to be in a valley at the bottom of the stunning snow-capped mountains, and even with it being the age of technology, cell phone service still doesn't work everywhere it needs to. I'm going to have to hoof it down the road a ways until I get some service bars on my phone and can call for a ride. I guess I should be glad it happened this early in the month, before a random blizzard hits and the snow's too deep to get my car out easily enough.

I turn off the radio because I need to concentrate and not distract myself by belting out festive lyrics. Now is not the time to be singing *Jingle Bell Rock,* when I'll be jingle bell freezing my tush off walking down the road. "Come on, Matilda, you can do this." I talk to my baby, rubbing the dashboard, then pop the gear into reverse. I give it a little gas, knowing you never gun the accelerator in a situation such as this. A sloshing sound fills the air, and my car goes nowhere. Not even an inch.

"Well, it was worth a try," I attempt to reason and put the gear back into park. There's no reason to get mad over something I have no control over, so it is what it is. See? That's my inner *holiday Zen* working already.

Spinning around, I reach between the seats, grabbing my coat, gloves, and hat. Thankfully, I learned early on to expect any kind of weather here, so I've packed my suitcase to be prepared. I'll have to leave my other belongings for now, but it's no big deal. I'll have it by tomorrow, I'm sure.

"Alright, it's going to be cold as icicles out there, and my nose will freeze, but it's okay. Everything is okay, I'm okay, the car's okay, this entire situation is a-o-kay." I keep talking to myself as I shift around, putting each arm inside my coat, then stuff my wallet into my inside pocket, and tug the front zipper all the way up to my chin. My favorite white beanie with puff on top goes next, and finally, my gloves. I stuff my cell into my coat pocket, zipping it for good measure, because I'm not about to take a chance of it falling out and me getting my tinsel in a tangle before I even arrive at my destination.

I'll ask Dad to stop by Tasty Sip for me on the way home. He'll order my favorite, along with something to snack on, and I'll be right as rain in a jiff.

The delicious thought is all the motivation I need to get me unbuckling my seatbelt and shutting the car off. I open my door and carefully step out. If I hit icy patches while driving, then I'm certain there will be plenty more around, and I'm not trying to biff it. I close the door with a sigh and click the lock button on my fob, making it beep, then stuff it in my opposite coat pocket. Once it's zipped closed as well, I keep one hand on the car and carefully make my way around the back.

And *scream*.

SAPPHIRE KNIGHT

CHAPTER TWO

WINTER

A massive man walks behind my car on his way to my side. His presence reminds me of a grumpy bear with his beanie pulled low, sturdy Carhart coat securely closed, low slung dark wash jeans, and snow boots. I'm having flashbacks from the movie *I Know What You Did Last Summer*, my mind quickly conjuring up a sharp ice pick for him to wield and all.

"Whoa," he holds his hands up, pausing before he can take another step. "Easy, Miss. I didn't mean to scare you; I just stopped to help."

I know that voice...

"I-I didn't see you. Or hear you, for that matter, and you've caught me off guard." I admit, taking him in from head to toe all over again. He's big everywhere, height, width, you name it, and I'd bet he's stacked with muscles underneath his cold-weather attire. I glance over his frame, silently chastising myself in the process because this is not the time to be checking the man out.

"Winter?" His mouth drops open, his icy-blue, sparkling gaze the one now skating over me. When we were younger, I always thought his irises looked more gray in the winter, rather than the signature blue every female reporter seems to comment on in their hockey reports. The color is so pale against the wintry white snow in the background right now that I'm pleased to note I'm still right.

"Sean?" I knew I was familiar with that voice from somewhere!

Too bad it has to belong to my *ex*. The one I gave my heart to a long time ago. The man who turned out to be a super-talented hockey star. The same guy who was just named GQ's man of the year. *Just great.*

I gaze at him, looking from a GQ spectator point of view. *Why does he have to look better in person?* Not that I bought the magazine or anything. I may've glanced at it online in my spare private time, however, wracking my brain if I'd ever considered him being the type of man to end up on a popular magazine cover. The answer was a resounding no, by the way.

"It really is you," he responds, his voice laced with a hint of softness.

Is he actually pleased to see me? It almost sounds like it, but that surely can't be the case. Not since he's the one who broke my heart a long time ago. I need to keep reminding myself so I'm not even a touch bitter about it. Now's not the time or place; it's the holidays, and I plan on holy-jollying my way through the next month.

"Yep, it's me. All in one piece," I reply awkwardly and cringe to myself. *Is that seriously the best I could come up with?* I've dreamt of getting a moment like this, never thinking it'd actually happen in my lifetime, but I must've played this scenario over in my mind a hundred times and never once lacked for a witty retort. "I mean...Hi, how are you, Sean?"

"Uh, I'm good." He nods, and I instantly feel a touch better. He's just as weird about this scenario as I am. "So you spun out, like old times, huh? I'm glad I stopped."

Is he truly glad it was him, or is he saying that to be kind? Also, who cares. All that matters is that he can give me a ride up the mountain to call someone, so I don't have to walk in the cold and snow after all.

"Yep, that's me, the spinner-outer. Um, would you mind driving me up the hill some so I can get enough cell service to call my dad? I need him to come get me and take care of my car."

"I just passed your family in the village, so they won't answer if you call your folks' house. How about I give you a ride home? If you'll unlock your car, I can snag your bags for you."

I click the key fob without argument, enjoying how his lips turn up just enough to flash me a dimple with his cute little smirk. I always swooned over that sucker when I was a teenager. If he really wanted to knock my socks off, he'd grin, and then I'd be toast for whatever else he happened to say. I swear, the man could talk himself out of anything wearing those dimples.

Sean Spruce was the town's good 'ol boy, going off to play hockey in the junior league and then again, on a full-ride scholarship. Only to end up making it big-time in the pros, getting paid more zeros than I could ever imagine spending. Of course, he could do no wrong in anyone's eyes back then, and I'm sure they think he now walks on water or something else just as ridiculous. Typical successful jock from a small town, you know how it goes.

He grabs my heavy, oversized suitcase and my big duffel bag, which had been taking up most of my back seat. He carries both of them like they weigh nothing while leading the way to his truck. The four-by-four is big and manly, trimmed out with some beefy tires and dark-tinted windows. He opens the passenger side door for me, because he's a gentleman like that and apparently hasn't forgotten some of the manners he was raised on.

"Thanks," I offer a smile and reach inside, attempting to climb in.

I place one foot on the side step, and in the next blink, I go sliding. My eyes clench closed as my arms flail, expecting to land on my butt in the snow. I momentarily brace for the sting to hit me from the impact, but it never happens. Instead, I find myself wrapped in a pair of very capable hands. His muscular arms hold me firmly enough that I'm definitely not going anywhere unless he puts me there. I sigh, because really? Of all the people for this to happen with, it has to be him.

"Oh my God! That was a close one," I whisper. I'm out of breath from the situation when I didn't really do anything at all.

"Mmhmm, how about you let me help you? I know you can do it yourself, but I don't want you to slip anymore and injure yourself."

His gentlemanly reasoning makes sense, so I nod and let him partially lift me into the truck. He does it so quickly and gracefully, I don't know it's happened until I'm safely sitting in the seat. I must still be in a bit of shock, because in the next moment, he grabs the seatbelt and reaches the belt across me, securely buckling me in.

"Thanks," I manage to respond. I'm feeling a bit breathless for a whole new reason now, my body tingling in every single spot his arm just brushed against. My mind's a bit fuzzy, like a cloud of happy warmth has just descended over me.

He smells good, too, like crisp, mountain man, if that were a smell. Pine, cloves, smoke, and snow all wrapped in one. It should be illegal for him to smell so divine when he already looks as handsome as he does and has a slice of charm to back it up. If there was any doubt in the back of my mind, it's gone now. I know the village has been treating this man like a king. At least I can be a little miffed over that, since I've been dubbed a troublemaker ever since the pasture incident happened.

"No problem." He winks and closes my door, moving to put my belongings in the back seat.

He just winked at me. *Winked!* Can you believe the nerve of this guy? I want to be appalled, but rather, I find myself still hazy over the entire interaction like a giant goober.

The driver's side door opens, and he hops up into the truck with practiced ease. Although with his height, it's probably like sliding into a car for me. The truck suits him; it fits with his overwhelming, yet understated presence. "You warm enough? I can turn the heat up?" He says it like a question, and I appreciate him making sure I'm comfortable.

I shake my head. He'd left his truck running when he came to check on me, so it's already cozy in here. "Are you here visiting your mom for Thanksgiving, or…" I trail off, hoping he'll fill in the rest, and put my nosiness to ease.

"Yeah, I was overdue for a visit. How about you? Looks like a lot of luggage for a quick trip."

I may've overpacked a little, but a girl can never have too many clothes or shoes, in my opinion. We're not like guys who are fine with the same three choices with a variety pack of underwear; we need options. "I'm home for a month. I was overdue, too."

"Interesting," he responds cryptically, but doesn't prod any further.

In no time, his oversized pick-up truck has us over the rest of the mountain and descending into the valley. My breath catches as I take in the village and the surrounding property; it's stunning, and I have to fight off tears from welling. I've missed this place since my last visit more than I realized. It's not that I'm miserable where I live; it's the opposite, actually, and I've been quite happy there. Until recently. As I've gotten older, I look around myself, noticing I'm missing out on the things I want to do the most. I've always aspired to be successful in business and work my tail off until I feel that I've reached a specific level. You know, burst my way through the glass ceiling and all of that jazz, but it's no longer as appealing as it once was.

I want to be able to enjoy life, not just work my way through it, while missing out on all the good stuff. There's so much I want to experience and also bring into my life that city living doesn't offer. Coming back home is like looking into a snow globe filled with so many things I want, but didn't realize until it was too late. I was in such a hurry to leave this place, I never anticipated I'd regret it and wish to be back.

As soon as I see the bars pop up on my cell again, I send a quick text to Samantha. I can't wait to see her.

Me: Just got into town. Tell your husband to hurry up and start his vacation! I need my BFF here already.

Me: Also, I've got some tea to tell ya… *wink emoji*

I close out of my text message, knowing the last one will pique her curiosity.

"Do you want me to stop anywhere so you can pick up anything before we get to the farm?"

I shake my head, not willing to prolong this visit with him any longer than I have to, even for a treat from Tasty Sip. "No, thank you. I appreciate the ride so much. Truly." I reply and barely glance at him. I keep my stare pinned on the road ahead of us or glance out the window on my side, smiling each time I see another deer. I can't risk looking over at him, or I may get stuck staring, and I've already been embarrassed enough for today; I don't want to add any more to it.

After a beat, I say, "I'll have to send over some of those cookies your mom always raves about as a thank you. I'm sure I won't see you before you head back, so it's the least I can do to repay you for giving me a lift."

He looks over at me long enough that I eventually meet his stare, ready to ask him why he's not paying attention to the road instead. His brow hikes, a smile curling his lips as he responds, "Your mom didn't tell you the news? About Thanksgiving?"

"Um, no?" I frown and shake my head, waiting for him to continue.

"Our moms have become even closer, basically best friends at this point. We're eating at your place for Thanksgiving dinner, so I'll be seeing you again day after tomorrow. Probably for most of your visit, actually, since they're always together."

Of course they are.

Chapter Three

SEAN

Of all the people to come across stuck on the side of the road, it had to be her. I should've been expecting it, but at the same time, I never would've thought she wouldn't be a seasoned driver by now. That she would know to avoid the snow piles. Once I got out of my truck and saw her face, the surprise hit me square in the chest of just how beautiful she's become. I always believed she was pretty when we were younger, but time has been kind to her as she's absolutely stunning.

I'd seen the tail end of the hunter green sedan sticking out of the piled-up snow along the side of the road as I was driving by and had immediately pulled over. Knowing it was the same car Winter drove the last time I saw her, and the *'what if it's really her'* scenario momentarily flashed through my mind. I'd waved it off, thinking she'd surely have a different vehicle by now, I mean, that was probably fifteen years ago, at least. Boy, was I wrong in assuming, and in my mistake, I'd been taken off guard the moment I saw her. She'd stared at me with those stunning hot cocoa-colored irises of hers, and the greeting I'd had on the tip of my tongue went quiet. Then she screamed, which made things awkward.

She always smelled so good, too, and having her scent lingering in my truck after I'd dropped her off stirred up even more memories we'd shared in the past. Once I'd admitted to her how I thought of her eyes as hot cocoa, she started wearing this intoxicating perfume that was a mixture of vanilla and marshmallow. You could put her next to a fire out in the cold with friends back in the day, and it was my favorite place to be. So imagine my surprise in discovering she's still wearing it…

It can't be because of me, right?

Having her in the seat next to me on the ride to the farm made me realize that it's been way too long since I've actually seen her in person. Of course, I've done the random social media recon when one of our mutuals would tag her in a 'visiting' post or something, but for the most part, I've tried to forget about her. I had no other choice, as she's the one who's had my heart all along, and I knew there was no way she'd take me back.

I may've been the one to turn away from us as a couple all those years ago and break up with her, but at the time, I thought I was doing the right thing. I had just accepted a scholarship to a college in another state, and at the time, I had no choice. I had several offers on the board, but I had to take the one the Pines agreed to let me play hockey at, since they basically owned my future.

There was also the fact that Dad had passed away when I was younger, and I knew at some point I'd probably need to step in and help Mom so she could eventually retire. It wasn't fair for her to be left with the debt Dad's passing caused, along with raising me alone, and I was determined to make sure she didn't struggle. In order to do that, I had to go to college for as long as I could, play the best hockey I'd ever played in my entire life, and work my butt off to finally get my signing bonus to the NHL. The Pines had signed me early, but I didn't see a cent until I actually walked on to the team and showed them that I could play at the pro level.

Little did I know, but Mom went back to school during the hours she wasn't busy working. She'd surprised me when she sent me an invitation to her graduation. She became a nurse all while still managing to consistently check on me and make me somehow feel as if I was the center of her attention at all times. I don't know how she did it, working full-time, going to school, and being a great long-distance mom, but she did. I'd asked her why she didn't tell me, and she had said it was because she didn't know if she could do it in the end, and didn't want to fail in front of me. I couldn't believe Mom would ever doubt herself, and at the time, it made me realize she's not the 'super mom' on a pedestal I've always believed she was. I gained so much new respect for her, showing her vulnerability and overcoming it in the process.

Other reasons pushed me to move away from Noel Falls and stop speaking to Winter as well. The first, namely being her grandfather. Winter and I hadn't been dating for very long at the time when I'd run into her grandfather in the village. I was crazy about her already at that point, and was in one of the small shops attempting to find her a sterling silver locket. I wanted to surprise her and get something engraved to make it an extra special gift. Even with us being young at the time, I'd already felt deep inside that she was different somehow.

Anyway, I'll never forget the look he'd given me when I'd told him about my plan and gift for his granddaughter. I was expecting a pat on the back and to be cheered on, that I was doing a good job of treating her sweetly before making it official and asking her to be my long-distance girlfriend while I went to college. I thought maybe she'd even want to come with me…

Instead, I got a lecture that hit me straight out of left field and had my chest aching as he went on to explain how easily Winter's mind could be influenced at her age. He was quite clear on her family's worries and how they all believed she'd give up on her dreams to follow me along, while I chased mine. I tried to make him see reason and explain how I'd never expect anything of the sort from her, but he was adamant in his beliefs, and that in the end…

I'd be the one to ruin her life.

There was no way I could allow myself to stand in her way of achieving whatever she wanted. My parents had raised me to believe that when you truly care for someone, you sacrifice if necessary. You let the person spread their wings and fly; never hold them back.

I did what was asked of me, no matter how much it bothered me. I ended our short relationship, and I quietly slipped away into the background. Then, I left for college, refusing to ever clip Winter's wings and to only set her free.

I can't say I nursed a huge heartache for long. Was I sad when I first pulled away from her? Of course. Like I mentioned, when Winter and I were together, I felt a deeper connection with her. It was probably way too strong and much too fast for it to be happening, but it never got the chance to fully blossom, and, in the end, I think I missed our friendship the most.

When I told her we couldn't be together anymore, she stopped speaking to me altogether. Not that I can blame her for it. If the roles had been reversed, I'd probably have done the same thing. At the time, I thought she hated me, so I left her alone. Now that I'm older and can look back at the situation, I can see she was hurting. If I could go back and do things differently, I would've kept trying to talk to her so she knew I was truly sorry, and we could've possibly remained friends over the years.

The spark between us is still there. I felt it the moment I looked into her eyes and then more strongly when she fell into my arms. It was as if she was meant to be there all along, and I was too foolish to shake myself out of my college stupor before being bogged down with studies and practices, to let myself ever remember. Then, my college time ran out, and the NHL quickly took over everything. Life just kept pushing me further and further away from Winter. Now, it's almost as if we're two strangers who have this overwhelming chemistry, but she's still too hurt from the past to acknowledge it, and would rather pretend she doesn't know me at all.

It's okay, we may not be *meant to be* together forever, or perhaps we are, and our meeting each other like this is *kismet*. Either way, I'm not making the same mistake as I did before. I plan to talk to her every chance I get. Maybe, just maybe, I can get her to stop seeing me as a bad guy and be able to have one of my friends back.

I'd love to have more time with her. I've never lost interest, in fact, but I don't know if she'd ever give me a true chance. Besides, I'm not sure if nursing a freshly broken heart is what I need over the holidays and then straight into the second half of our season, if she were to turn me down.

I silently send up thanks that I have my strict practice schedule to keep up with while I'm at home, and that I keep up with it, because there's a chance she never would've gotten a ride had I not been on my way. Some of my teammates like to say that I go too hard on our days off, even when we're supposed to be resting and relaxing with our families, but I can't help it. Hockey has given me everything I have in life, including the nice-sized nest egg I've set aside for whenever Mom decides to hang up her scrubs and retire. I want her to be comfortable, so I work hard for my high-paying contracts and signing bonuses.

I've also been setting some of my money aside in stocks and bonds for whatever I plan to do in the second half of my life, as well as investing in small start-up businesses that have struggled and been denied by banks. My time is coming up, and I know retirement is just a year or two away, most likely. If I were a goalie, for example, I'd still have another five or ten years left in me, but I'm not that lucky.

Since I'm not protected as much in my gear and take a lot of hits, injuries are unavoidable, and I know it's just a matter of time before a fresh-faced rookie comes in and claims my spot. I'm not bitter about it, truly. I've had my time in the spotlight with a successful career and stats, so when the time does finally come, I can embrace it with class. I think the hardest part, aside from not being on the ice with a team, is deciding what to do after. I'm hoping that with me being home around Mom, she can help guide me a little as to where my focus should be for those next steps. I figure if anyone in the world knows me best and can help me decide, it's her.

Releasing a breath, I set my gear down in the laundry room and take my shoes off. Even being in my thirties, I know better than to push my luck with walking through the house carrying stinky equipment in my dirty boots. "Hey, Mom, I'm back. Gonna shower then I'll be down," I yell by way of greeting, then quickly take the steps leading up to the second story and to my room. It's my childhood home, but thankfully, Mom took mercy on me and removed all the posters and every other teenage piece of me out of my room. Now, it's my home away from my apartment, the place I can turn my cell off and relax.

I make my way into the living room after I've washed and thrown on a fresh pair of sweats. The fire's roaring in the fireplace, which reminds me I still need to head outside and chop some more wood. I try to keep Mom stocked up with every trip I make here, so she never has to worry about it and doesn't end up hurting herself trying to be a lumberjack on top of everything else she does. The woman never stops going, but I guess staying busy keeps her happy.

"Mom?"

"Hey, Sean. I'm in here," she calls from the kitchen. I find her at the counter with sandwich stuff spread everywhere. "Hungry?"

I nod. With all of my training, I'm basically a bottomless pit. "Starving." I immediately jump in beside her, assembling my club sandwich while she makes hers. "Fresh bread?"

"Yep. I'd love to claim that I'm the one who baked it, but it was Brenda."

"Brenda, as in Winter's mom?" I clarify, because there are three Brendas who live in town.

She nods. "Mmhm. She makes the best sourdough around, although I don't know how she finds the time to do it." She laughs and picks up her sandwich, taking a big bite while leaning her hip against the counter.

I copy her by taking a bite and resting my back against the counter. It feels good on the lower lumbar, where I always seem to be sore these days. "Mm. Good idea on the sandwich."

"Right? Told you." She takes another bite before asking, "Did you get the stuff from the store I'd asked you to, while you were in Noelville?"

It's the closest city to Noel Falls, hence the names being nearly the same to each other. Noelville is small compared to most cities, but big enough that they have the chain grocery stores and the only professional hockey rink within a hundred-mile radius. "Of course. I did forget the bags in my truck, though, so I'll have to run out after I eat this. I still need to go outside and take care of some more wood for you anyhow."

"How did I get so lucky to have a son like you?"

I shrug, flashing a smile full of sandwich like I used to do as a teen, making her groan with disgust. I cover my mouth, laughing. After I chew and swallow, I confess, "I found a car nearly in the ditch on my way home."

"Oh yeah? Anyone we know?"

"Winter."

Her eyes light up, her lips tipping into a small smile. "Her mother told me she'd be here for the holidays. Supposedly, she'll be in town for a full month. I have a feeling that later on today, when she discovers her father hurt himself and can't work the farm much, she'll be staying even longer. I understand they didn't want to worry Winter and have her drive all this way through the snow while distracted, but at the same time…"

"They should've told her right away," I finish for her, thinking the same thing, and she nods. "Yeah. Not gonna lie, I'd be pretty upset if something happened to you and I wasn't notified right away. I'd want to come home and help out if I could, snow or no snow on the ground."

"I would never do that to you, not after Daddy."

She doesn't have to say it out loud. My father's passing away suddenly affected both of us strongly, and it still makes my heart hurt. He was a good man and a great father. He's the reason why I fell in love with hockey in the first place. He would be out on the ice with me every chance he had at the local ice rink when he wasn't working. He taught me skating drills and little tricks he swore would make me faster. He'd shown me the best way to sink the puck in the net, along with how to take criticism from other players and let it roll on one shoulder and right off the other.

Not only did he share his love for hockey with me, but he took pride in teaching me things I'd need to know as a man someday. Fishing, hunting, chopping wood, replacing a tire, a truck battery, a leaky dishwasher, taking Mom flowers, and more. You name it, and the man figured out a way to fix it with me being his sidekick. He was my best friend, and every day since he passed away, there has been a hole in my heart the size of Niagara Falls from where he's meant to be.

"Winter hasn't changed much. Do you know what she's been up to? Married?"

Mom smirks at my question, shaking her head. She's mentioned Winter a few times on the phone in passing, but I've always acted like I wasn't interested. After seeing her, well, let's just say I'm interested.

In absolutely everything, where she's concerned.

"Not married. Never married, in fact. No kids, yet. According to Brenda, she wants them, but hasn't found the right person." She takes another bite and chews for a moment.

She continues, "I think she's a workaholic like you are. Brenda's always worried about her being so busy that she burns herself out. This visit home will do their whole family good, that I'm sure of. Besides, it'll be nice seeing her around the village. It's about time she comes home for good."

My brows skyrocket as I lowly whistle. "Home for good? You're putting some weight on those words, Mom. You sure she's on board with this, too?"

She shrugs. "I'm not. I'm only hoping she sees that her family needs her, and the time ends up being right for her, too. You know how we are around here; we love to watch our community be successful in whatever life they choose, but we also enjoy having them come home and rejoin the community at some point. Noel Falls has always been one big family, and anyone coming back into the fold is always welcomed with open arms."

She's laying this on a little thick, making me think she's not only talking about Winter, but possibly is hinting at me, too. *Does Mom want me to give up my hockey career and come home for good? What would I even do here?* These thoughts are exactly what I'm hoping she can help guide me with.

"Anyway," she breaks up my thoughts. "You ready for Thanksgiving? You'll see Winter again when we go over to join her family for dinner and the day."

"Yeah, uh, I thought we were just eating over there. What do you mean by *the day*?"

"Oh, Son, you know how these holidays are." She puts the sandwich stuff away, finally turning to me and tossing me a water bottle. I catch it, of course, and take our dirty plates and napkins, throwing them in the trash. "Football, playing cards, turkey, dessert, laughter, and good old-fashioned fun with friends."

I went from teasing Winter that I'd see her for Thanksgiving dinner, to momentarily panicking now at realizing that I'll also be spending the day with her.

What should I wear?

What am I going to say?

Will she even speak to me?

Chapter Four

Winter

"Oh, you guys are in so much trouble," I grumble as my parents finally return home. I'm thinking this constitutes coal in the stocking. I don't care that they had my favorite hot chocolate and peppermint syrup waiting for me on the counter when I arrived; they are in deep. That was bribe hot cocoa, and I'm not falling for it for a second.

Gram gasps, hand flying to her mouth in outrage. Pops huffs and continues reading his newspaper. Dad groans, covering his eyes with his hand but spreading his fingers enough to meet my disappointed gaze.

Mom shoots me a perturbed look while shaking her head. "Really, Winter? Coal in our stockings?"

"Yep, I said it. I went there. This is pretty big on the naughty scale, especially from my own family. Dad is seriously hurt, and you all kept it from me? I could see if it happened yesterday, but the poor man has been injured for three weeks! Does Holly know?" I ask, with my brows nearly in my hairline, my hand resting on my hip, and of course, my hip jutted out in added exclamation, too.

This is outrageous.

I swear, if my sister knows and hasn't told me, she's in for a Christmas surprise, namely being on my naughty list.

"Oh, honey," Dad sighs, adjusting his leg.

It's in a massive cast. When the man falls from a horse on the farm, he doesn't just fracture a wrist; he goes for the whole shebang. Broken leg, basically from top to bottom, broken elbow, and broken collarbone. He is literally out of order from top to bottom. I'm outraged over this and with good reason.

My family has obviously been juggling taking care of the animals, and I'd bet that no one has started preparing the honey for the holiday markets. We make candles, body whip, decorative jarred honey, honey candy, honey soap, you name it, and we basically make it with our farm's honey. It's the busiest time of the year aside from when the animals are having babies, and we're looking at not making a cent for the farm for winter. All because of my family's need to meddle by not wanting to worry me before I could officially take off from work and visit.

Unbelievable!

"Dad, seriously? You know I would've gotten out of work sooner somehow to help you. This is our family's farm; we all pitch in when needed, and this is no different." I tear up, unable to stop myself from becoming overly emotional. I can't stand to see my father hurt this badly when he is the best man I know. He does so much for others, especially those in the community, and for this to happen, it really puts my stocking in a fire.

"I know you would've, and that's exactly why I didn't call you. I don't need my daughters here worrying about me, fussing around when they have their own lives to live. Besides, we wanted to spend Christmas with you, and knew you wouldn't be able to take time off for both occasions."

As if his breaking several bones constitutes as an *occasion*. It's a very important medical emergency. "Hm, so I guess this means you haven't told Holly yet?"

My mom shakes her head, and I furrow my brow, frowning at her. She's a medical doctor; she should want my sister and me here to help him around and with the farm. "We've been getting by, making sure the animals are fed and kept warm with the early snowfall. Besides, your sister is in France. It's not like she can pick up and go whenever she feels like it."

Oh, it's exactly like that. My older brother, Dasher, is in the military, so I'm not expecting him to be able to leave at a moment's notice. However, Holly and I have no excuse. Besides, I know my brother would still do his best to get some leave time approved to come help out around here. We'd do anything for our parents.

"Mom," I say, and immediately tug my cell from my back pocket and hit the speed dial number I have programmed for my sister. "This has to end now. Does Dasher know?"

Pops peeks around the side of his newspaper, "He sure does."

My hand flies up in a 'really?' motion, and I watch as the video call to my sister rings and rings, without her picking up. "She's probably sleeping or something, but just so you know, the jig is up, and I'm telling everyone who doesn't know. We all love you, and if my siblings can't get here in time to help out, the least they can do is pray daily for your health."

Mom and Dad both nod, knowing I'm getting my way on this one.

Gram's lips twist into a smirk, "Noticed your car's missing, Winter. How'd you get home?" She's a nosey old bat, but she always has been.

I sigh, remembering my car is on the side of the road in a giant pile of snow and most likely will be stuck there for a while after seeing Dad in his casts. I was really looking forward to him driving the tractor down the hill to get me unstuck, but I guess that won't be happening anytime soon. The tractor doesn't have any working heat inside, or I'd be attempting to do it myself, but even I'm not that crazy.

"Speaking of my car." I sigh again, then admit, "I hit a couple patches of ice." Now it's my turn to wince, knowing my family will not be surprised to hear the news. I'm a good driver, really, I am. I just have a tendency to run off the road at times, but no one has ever been hurt, thankfully.

"Oh, no! Are you okay?" Mom heads for me, wearing her doctor look, ready to check me over.

My siblings and I never got a fake sick day growing up because the woman is too smart for her own good. It was rough being one of those kids who were awarded perfect attendance while everyone else snickered because they got extra days off. We had to come up with more creative ways to get out of going to school all the time, like joining every club under the sun. My brother played every single sport he could, and my sister was too busy being a smarty pants and graduated early. Me, on the other hand, I was involved with the community and had my best friend, Samantha, around to steal me away to attend games and stuff. Hence, how I became so involved with the holiday festival, which was always my favorite activity to volunteer for.

I hold up my hand with a smile, attempting to show her I'm unharmed. "I'm fine, really. Not even a neck jerk or anything. I promise. I will tell you if I feel even a twitch of discomfort."

"Thank heavens. You didn't walk home, did you? Please tell me you're too stubborn for that."

I roll my eyes and shake my head. Of course, I'm too stubborn. Has she drunk too much eggnog already? There's no way I was going to hoof it the entire way home in the *freezing* cold. "No, I didn't walk. Sean Spruce happened to be driving by and saw my car on the side of the road. He stopped to help, and said he'd seen you all in town, so he gave me a ride home."

Gram's nose twinkles in a way telling me she's full of mischief, like always. The woman has been up to something from the moment I was old enough to realize she's a bit of a troublemaker. Not in a bad way, she just meddles. And drinks Brandy when she shouldn't be. Take, for example, how she got my parents to go on their first date, or how she had every girl in town nearly proposing to my brother once he was old enough to marry.

"Such a nice young man, that Sean Spruce is." She voices her approval. "A true gentleman stopping to save you in your time of need."

Pop flicks his stare at her momentarily but remains quiet, quickly going back to his paper. I didn't know they even printed the newspaper around here anymore. I should get him a tablet for Christmas so he can read whatever news he wants.

I nod at Gram, having nothing to say in response but also knowing that rolling my eyes again is not the right answer at the moment. Yes, it was very kind of Sean to make sure I'm okay. It still doesn't mean I want to give him a gold medal or anything. It's not like the guy dug my car out with his bare hands and delivered it or anything.

Mom chooses this moment to share that she already knew he was here in town, and oh yeah, she must've forgotten to mention it to me, also. *Great, who needs a heads up with a man like him anyhow? Just take me out with a snowplow while we're at it.*

"Yes, Calla was counting the days down until he got enough of a break between his international schedule to visit. You know, they just finished playing a series of games in Canada. Anyhow, she said he has a few games between now and Christmas, and of course, a ton of practice. I guess he had to get special permission from his team to practice at the Noelville Blizzards rink while he travels back and forth between Noel Falls and New York with his current team, the Pines."

I'm very aware of what team he plays for. I've watched his games countless times. Yet, I'll never admit I've done so willingly. As far as anyone is concerned, I only watch Sean Spruce glide across the ice like he was born for it when Dad has it on TV with the volume blaring. He thinks Mom won't hear us shouting and cheering if the volume's up high enough, but she's got ears like a hawk.

She knows all of this, yet had somehow failed to mention a single word the last time we video chatted before I left the comfort of my apartment. "I heard you and his mom are closer friends now."

They've always been friends, but apparently, they're *besties attached at the hip* at this point, and I appear to know nothing at this rate. You'd think I've been gone for years, not a couple of months. Part of me wonders if I should see if my bedroom is still set up or if they've gone and changed that on me, too. Maybe they're hiding another kid they spontaneously decided to adopt or something around here, there's no telling, but these people need to take it down a notch.

She nods, beaming brightly. "Yes, she's over here all the time. Plus, we work together most days. I was so happy when she and Sean agreed to join us for Thanksgiving. There's nothing like having family around the dinner table, giving thanks, and spending the day together."

Wait, the day? And whose family? Because last time I checked, Sean and I are in no way related. Which I'm extremely thankful for because no matter how much it still hurts to see him on TV or in town, I still want to climb the man like a Lindt chocolate Christmas tree. Just thinking of having him here, in my space, has me needing to fan myself, and I'm not a twitterpated type of woman, trust me. I'm cool as a Christmas peppermint martini with a chocolate sprinkled sugared rim, but when he's around, I can't remember my own name, let alone be blasé about the entire situation.

I thought it was only for dinner.

My voice is a bit high-pitched, my heart thundering in my chest as I double check, "They're, uh, staying the entire day?" I go from sweet mint julep to cinnamon red hot in a flash, from momentarily picturing him licking his fork clean while sitting across from me at the family table. As Sam would say, *this is no bueno*. The turkey won't be the only thing getting cooked if I have to sit through that scenario for long.

"Of course. You know how we do the holidays around here. It's never *just* the food."

I nearly groan out loud, but manage to hold myself back.

Grams is silently laughing to herself over in the chair, and I'd bet the old bat knows way too much for her own good, just like my mother. She's tickled plum pink to see me squirm in place, silently stewing over the latest development. I'm sure this is playing right into the *hero image* she has of Sean. The man can play some good hockey, but it certainly doesn't make him a God or anything. It's not like he's out here scaling trees to save kittens or anything. Everyone in the village can skate at least a little bit, and Grams needs to remember as much. Next thing I know, she'll be trying to schedule dates for us to meet up, and I'm trying to stay as far away as possible from the Pines' number eleven.

I watch as Gram gets up and helps herself to another glass of eggnog. She sprinkles some cinnamon on top like she's here for the flavor and not the half a bottle of booze I'd bet my right boob on that she's spiked it with. I'll have to start my morning out with a glass on Thanksgiving; maybe it'll make the day go by smoothly. It'll be fuzzier, of that I'm sure of.

"Does anyone have a holly jolly Xanax we can spike the turkey with?" I ask, smirking as Gram cackles. Pop mutters something to himself, while Dad quietly chuckles with amusement. Mom ignores my comment completely, busying herself with putting another log on the fire.

"Did Samantha get to come home for Thanksgiving?" She asks, not paying attention to my current displeased frown as I think over my ex joining us for the holiday, and how I'd prefer to wear my stretchy pants and a loose shirt for turkey day whenever possible. It's the one time of the year we make it a sport of gorging ourselves and then chilling on the couch, and now I'm going to be stuck in dressy clothes for the day while being acutely aware of his proximity for the entire time.

Not good. I wonder if I can get him to cancel? Maybe puncture a tire on his snazzy truck?

"Winter?" She says my name, noticing I'd momentarily tuned out.

I try to think of what I missed and realize she's talking about Sam. My best friend since the first day we were in kindergarten, when Martin Mckindly said he didn't want me to sit by him, and Samantha loudly claimed I was sitting beside her for the entire year instead. *Instant best friends.*

"No, her husband had to work. She'll get to come for Christmas, though." And I absolutely can't wait. I miss her too much. She's got these two adorable kids and the nicest husband. I was her maid of honor when she married him, and I've never seen her happier. I just wish we lived closer to each other like we did growing up. Her mom's house is a quick fifteen-minute walk from here, a trail we used growing up, more times than I can count.

"Alright. Now that the fuss is all over, we're heading home. Winter can take it from here; we're calling it an early night." Pop declares, setting the paper down while getting to his feet. He and Gram live on the property, about a ten-minute walk or so from here.

I hug them both at the door on their way out, while promising I'll check on the animals before bed for Dad.

Facing my parents once the room is quiet, aside from the random crackle and pop from the large fireplace, I ask, "So, what's the plan for the festival?"

Mom glances away, suddenly having nothing to add, all the while Dad looks like a deer caught in headlights. He finally admits, "About the festival, it's too much work. I'm sorry, Winter, but I can't ask that of your grandparents, and Mom has her patients she's busy with. I couldn't get things started like I'd planned once I was injured."

Tears crest and quickly fall over my cheeks, making the room grow blurry. I was right, I should've been here. If I had only taken a job closer to home, then this possibly never would've happened, and if it had, at least I would've been able to come and go without hours of distance between us. In the past, we'd always start prepping what we could on November first. I'm twenty-six days late already, and I still have to help around the farm, so it's not as if I can dedicate all my time to getting everything ready.

Not gonna lie, I'm feeling a bit hopeless about having enough time to be able to pull this off. I can't ask anyone around town like we normally would be able to, because they're all prepping for the holidays too. Rather than spiral in silence, I spend the evening catching up with my parents and making the rounds around our farm, checking on all the animals.

Eventually, I climb into bed, exhausted from the day, and drift off into a restless sleep.

SAPPHIRE KNIGHT

Chapter Five

Winter

    I'm hurrying out of the Tasty Sip the next morning, hands full with large red and green cups of cappuccino, since they've already run out of their seasonal fall-colored cups. One's vanilla-flavored and topped with homemade whipped cream, caramel drizzle, and a cinnamon stick that I can't wait to try. The other's my favorite chocolate peppermint cappuccino topped with whipped cream, crushed candy canes, and holiday spirit. I also have a bag tucked under my arm filled with two cherry turnovers, but my Dad and I will have to eat them and hide the evidence before Gram catches sight of the sugary goodness, or we'll never hear the end of it. We all know her turnovers are the best in town; however, we also know she only makes them for special occasions, and we have to get our sweet pastry fix somehow.

I had to get over here first thing for my caffeine and sugar fix. I especially needed it after last night. I tossed and turned all night, dozing off only to wake up a million times. I kept having these crazy dreams. The first one was of a certain hockey player who will not be named. Anyway, he was following me around as I decorated trees, busily taking all the ornaments off behind me. When I confronted him about it, he'd smile and tell me I was on the naughty list with him. Then, in another dream, I was at the festival, but my booth was empty, and everyone kept walking by pointing and laughing at me.

Needless to say, I woke up a frazzled mess. I immediately took a hot shower and found my most fall-ish outfit. My sweater is beige, warm, and soft, which I expertly paired with some olive-colored jeans that have a lot of stretch in them. I added an olive, navy, and beige scarf to pull the colors together, along with my camel boots that're trimmed in light fur that also match my coat. If I were in the city, I'd look like everyone else my age. Here, I'm a touch more on the fashion-chic side and at least appear like I have my life together when today it feels like it may be falling apart unless I can somehow pull everything off that I need to.

My back to the shop's door as I use it to shove the glass door open and make my way out into the crisp, chilly air. Winter has hit Noel Falls just in time for Thanksgiving, and there isn't a doubt in my mind that it wasn't a random snowfall hitting early. Nope, I'd wager it's here to stay. I'm nodding to myself, eager to take a sip of my delicious hot beverage, when I venture onto the sidewalk without looking first and run smack into a wide, hard chest.

My drinks smoosh and spill all over said chest, and I instantly jump back. "Oh my God! I'm *so* sorry," I'm already apologizing before I glance up. Only to look straight into the eyes of my ex, Mr. GQ, himself.

I sigh, feeling the cold air kiss my skin everywhere the hot beverages have trailed over my hands. "No, no, no, this isn't happening," I mutter as I shake my head in denial.

Where's a boulder to crawl under when I need one? How is it that every time I see this guy, my life looks like it's a complete mess? "I'll buy you a new shirt, I swear. *OhmyGod, are you okay*?" I continue to ramble, mortified, and silently praying I didn't just give the local hockey hero third-degree burns that the town will shun me for.

"I'm okay. The cold out here, along with my jacket, is helping to take the brunt of it." His hands are holding my wrists, and I can't help but glance down at how big they seem while wrapped around my wrists as he holds me in place. It's almost as if he were going to be the one to catch me if I had fallen. Of course, he was. Local hometown hero, remember? I should expect nothing less.

I don't appreciate how responsive my body is to him in this proximity either. Not only is he handsome, but now I know he tastes like my favorite beverage, too. You know, if I were to taste him, that is. Gah, I can't believe I just went there when he's covered in liquid sugar.

"I'll get your jacket cleaned. I truly am sorry." I promise, while moving out of his hold and over to the nearest trash can by the entrance of Tasty Sip. With a frown firmly in place, I dump the empty cups, lids, and ruined turnovers, silently pouting that they were the last two available this morning. I shouldn't be mourning the pastries right now; it's neither the time nor the place, but I can't help it as my stomach loudly grumbles with hunger.

He smirks at the sound, his gaze playful. He makes it a point to inhale deeply before commenting, "By the smell, I'd guess you still have the same favorite? Large chocolate peppermint cappuccino topped with whipped cream and crushed candy canes?"

"And holiday spirit," I mumble. My cheeks pink for an entirely different reason that I may conveniently blame on the weather.

He chuckles, "Ah, right. How could I forget the sprinkles and mini marshmallows? Let's head in and get you another drink, now that I've ruined your morning fix."

"Oh, please, I'm the one who has probably ruined yours. The coffee is on me," I offer. Although I don't know why I bother, the guy is a professional hockey player and makes a ton of money. Dad saw a few articles on contract negotiations happening with Sean and his current team a while back, which he may have mentioned in passing a time or two. Apparently, the big bucks aren't going to the new rookie players, but to the well-oiled veterans who make the Pines plenty of money. This is all according to my father.

We head inside, and it doesn't go unnoticed that he holds the door open for me and then also for Mrs. Jacolby, wishing her a Happy Thanksgiving on her way out. I use the much-needed quick distraction to immediately go for a pile of napkins. Grabbing a handful, I clean my sticky fingers first and then turn to the big guy. My hands are on him in the next blink, dabbing, brushing, and eventually lifting the jacket material to see if it's wet underneath to wipe, before it hits me what I'm doing. I'd lifted his shirt accidentally, too, in my rush, and I managed to get an eyeful of bare skin. Let me just say, the man obviously doesn't miss a workout. I can't believe he even drinks coffee with the firm stomach I just got a glimpse of.

Well, now I'm going to have to fight myself from salivating over him all over again, since my mind won't stop picturing the light outline of his abs. Nor the dark sprinkle of hair leading lower. And those hips. Christ on a cracker, the man has those hip muscle thingies that pop out and drive women wild. This is exactly not what I need to be seeing or thinking of, since I'll have him in my home all day tomorrow and will have to play it off like I'm unruffled the entire time.

Taking a step back, I offer him a sheepish grin and drop the material of his jacket and shirt. I hold the wad of napkins out, "Here. Um, in case I, uh, missed some," I offer, feeling like I'm in third grade with my first crush and we're trading pudding cups at lunch time. Seriously, though, who can blame me? The guy is insanely gorgeous. Dimples. Sparkling eyes. Messy but styled hair. Windblown cheeks.

Gah, he's sort of beautiful for a man, and so tall. He's got those *good-good* genes.

"Thanks." He unzips his jacket, pulling the material off and somehow in the process making it look like a noteworthy task. I bet he does the reach behind tug-thingy guys do when removing their shirts, too. How do they even manage it? I've tried but nearly choked myself in the process. Thankfully, no one was around to bear witness to one of my many shenanigans I do for research purposes.

"What would you like?" I ask, gesturing to the giant chalkboard menu on the wall behind the main counter. Although I can still remember his order as if it were yesterday. I won't be admitting as much to him, though, especially since I seem to stick my foot in my mouth every chance I get where he's concerned. I'm desperately trying to come off as nonchalant as possible, considering he seems to take everything in stride, handling my chaos as it comes.

He smiles at Janet as she stands behind the counter and tells her, "Large Americano for me, please."

"I'll have a repeat of my last order. I accidentally dumped mine on Sean," I explain, gesturing to the man behind me.

I tug my phone from my back pocket to grab my debit card out of the attached card holder while Janet makes our drinks. A moment later, she sets them on the counter and then takes my card, swiping it. She's in the middle of telling Sean what fresh-baked goods she'll have at her booth on the opening night of the festival when the card machine makes a loud beep.

She meets my gaze, brow furrowed. "Hey, sweetie, your card says it's been declined." She's not being rude; she's Mom's age and has known me my entire life, so I don't mind her calling me sweetie.

Back to her question… *there's no way*. "That can't be right. Please swipe it again for me."

"Sure thing," she does as asked, and a beat later, the obnoxious beeping sound happens again. She shakes her head, but it's not necessary. The entire coffee shop and its patrons have a front row seat to my morning of shame and already know my card has been declined at this point.

"I got this one," Sean quickly offers as he reaches over my shoulder, holding out his shiny black card. He leans so close, I can feel his warmth on my back, and my toes curl in my boots. I get a whiff of his signature scent, and it's enough to make me momentarily dizzy with how good it smells.

Janet hands me my dead plastic back, and I decide right here and now I'd like the ground to open up and swallow me whole. I was so *merry* on my way into town, but things are quickly going to hell in a handbasket at this rate. There's no way I'm spending my vacation at home being miserable when there's no place I'd rather be for the holidays. I have to remind myself of the things I'm thankful for and what this season truly encompasses. Goodwill, kindness, and love toward others. I can do this.

"Thank you," I tell him, while grabbing my fresh cappuccinos. "I'm sorry again, but this time for not being able to cover the coffee. I don't know if my card is frozen from traveling out of town, or what is going on with it." I admit and then set my two large cups down on the only free table in front of the windows.

I tug my cell free as he follows me. "Bring your jacket to my parents' house any time, and I'll clean it for you. I hope I didn't mess your day up too badly." I flash him a small smile, hopeful that I look remorseful, and then turn away. I'm expecting that to be the end of our interaction today, and for him to leave and do whatever he was planning to accomplish before I nearly burned the poor man's skin off first thing in the morning. I immediately pull up my banking app on my cell since the service is good right here, and attempt to figure out what's happening with my account. I'm engrossed in the transaction history, ignoring everyone around me, when the chair across from me at my same table is pulled out, and then Sean's large, overpowering presence fills the space.

He meets my stare, "Sit with me for a minute and tell me what has you up this early, and on the hunt for extra caffeine? Or did I read this wrong and you're taking coffee to your father?"

I shake my head while keying in my password. "No, he had his already. I was craving the extra sweet stuff today. I have a lot of work ahead of me and need the sugar and caffeine jolt." I leave out the part about dreaming of him all night long, especially since I was nearly petting his stomach earlier.

The app takes forever to load, making me sigh in frustration. My bars will drop if I leave, so I'm not going anywhere at the moment. I move the closest chair back just enough until I can squeeze in the space and sit. My gaze stays still locked on my phone as my account information finally pops up, then my mouth drops open in utter shock.

A strange noise leaves me, that's a cross somewhere between a woosh, from the air leaving my lungs, to a desperate cry of disbelief.

Chapter Six

SEAN

"Winter? What is it?" I question as she stares at her phone, disbelief and heartbreak written all over her face. I hate seeing her so torn, and her crestfallen expression has my heart beating a million miles an hour, and not in the good sort of way. I'm panicking inside, wondering how on earth I can get that look off her face immediately. How I can possibly help without her turning me away, because let's be real, she's always been a bit headstrong.

"I-it's my a-account," she quietly stammers, her lower lip trembling.

The last time I saw that lip shake was when I told her I couldn't see her anymore, that I was moving away without her. Witnessing it again is breaking my heart, not being able to stop it.

"Everything is *gone*, it's completely empty! Actually, it's overdrawn now, from my coffee charge earlier."

I reach across the table, my hand landing on top of hers as I lean in to take a look at her screen. It's none of my business, but I can't seem to help myself where this woman is concerned, and so help me, but I want to be in the middle of whatever she'll allow. "You were supposed to have money in there?" I dumbly ask. It's the wrong thing to say, as she suddenly bursts into tears. She's in emotional distress, and I'm the idiot asking if her bank account is supposed to have money in it. Of course it is. "Wait, back up. I didn't mean for it to come out like that."

She taps on a few arrows on her screen, expanding each item, then she shakes her head. "Someone must've stolen my information. There are several charges on my bank card not from me, and they've drained every single penny all in the matter of a few minutes. I had over five thousand dollars saved in there!"

I rack my mind for what could've happened, and then it hits me. The warning my bank always emailed out to its account holders, especially around the holidays. "Did you fill up with gas on your way here and pay at the pump somewhere?" I'm asking as I reach for the napkin dispenser and offer her a few for her tears and sniffles. I'd love more than anything to gently wipe her tears with my thumbs, but I doubt very much she'd tolerate it at a moment like this.

She nods, brow furrowed at what probably sounds like a random question. "Yeah, and I even went inside to use the bathroom and grab a drink. Why?"

I continue, "Call your bank and tell them. More than likely, a thief had a card reader on the gas pump and stole your card information. Thieves and scammers do it all the time; my bank sends us several warnings per year about how to avoid it."

"Part of that money is for my rent next week. What am I going to do?"

She's still crying, her tears silent but loud all in the same, and I feel terrible, I'm not putting her at ease in any way. It seems she's on a streak of tough luck since I've seen her, but I won't point that out. I'm sure it'll only upset her further.

I lay my hand back on top of hers again, knowing I should move it away, but I don't want to. I haven't earned the right to touch her, yet, but whenever she's around, I can't seem to stop myself. "We'll make a plan." I suggest and take a sip of my coffee before continuing, "First things first. Call the bank. Then, call your landlord next, and tell them what's happened with your account. Ask for a temporary extension, and pick whatever date is furthest that they'll offer you, so you have plenty of time. When do you get paid next?"

She shakes her head, teeth sunk into that luscious lower lip, and in any other situation I'd want to pull it free, but there's a time and place for it, and the Tipsy Sip is not it. "I just got paid two weeks ago, on top of what I was able to save after I did some of my Christmas shopping, and I had just enough cash in my bank to cover my other expenses while I took time off. You don't understand how bad this is..." She pauses, glancing around, and then finally takes a sip of her drink.

I'd bet there's a silent war going on inside her head right now as she decides what she will and won't share with me. I remember there once was a time she didn't hesitate to confide in me, and a pang hits me straight in the chest over her not feeling the same sense of safety with me in this moment. I could fix this right here and now if she'd let me, but I know it's merely wishful thinking and she won't allow it.

"Talk to me, Winter Wonderland." I revert to one of the nicknames I called her when we were younger, hoping it helps her feel comfortable enough to open up. "Let me help shoulder this burden you're obviously carrying around inside. You know it'll help talking through it."

We stare at each other for a moment, silent, with both of us too stubborn and generally helpful to back down and close off this conversation. She's upset, and if I can solve it somehow, I want to. Finally, she takes another drink of her sugar overload confection and divulges, "I can't go back to work early. I don't know if you've already heard, but my dad is hurt pretty badly. I have to work the farm for him. We're already behind schedule on festival prep, which is why I was in here in the first place. I need all the extra energy I can get because I'm supposed to start on it all today."

My coffee's long forgotten now, as I admit my mom has filled me in a little bit. "Mom mentioned he was injured falling off his horse. She's taken dinner over a few times for your folks when your mom had to work a long shift at the clinic. She didn't tell me much past that, you know, with patient confidentiality and all. I'm sure people around town know by now, too, but I'm not one to pay attention to their gossip."

"Oh, God," she bursts out suddenly. Her eyes grow wide as she rushes to say, "My parents can't know about this, okay? If they find out my account has been drained and I'm panicking, they'll insist on my going back home early. I can't let that happen when they obviously need me here. They're selfless enough that they will suffer in silence, so I won't have to worry about my bills, but I absolutely can't allow it to happen."

I nod, already agreeing with her. "You got it, I won't utter a word. This conversation is between you and me, and if anyone talks about it, I'll shut them down on the spot," I promise with a protective growl, flashing my determined stare at each of our nosy table neighbors. I have no doubt they've all seen my games, so they'll know firsthand how well I can smash people into the walls around the rink if they get in my way. Hopefully, it's enough to keep their tongues from wagging and this information from eventually getting back to her family.

As for the bank issues she's having, I know there's no way she'll let me give her any money. All I can do right now is hope the bank ends up reversing the fraudulent charges and gives her the funds back so she can forget all of this ever happened in the first place. Otherwise, I can listen and try to help out however she'll allow it, but I doubt it'll be much. Tomorrow is Thanksgiving, so I'll be seeing her again when Mom and I go to her parents' place.

That's it!

I'll wait until we're eating dinner with everyone around us. I'll bring up how the farm and festival are a lot of work, and then innocently suggest to the table that I help her out in my off time. It won't be much since I have to practice and travel for some games, but it's one way I can pitch in to help shoulder some of the load off of her. I know if the bank doesn't return her money, she'll be completely stressed out trying to navigate it all on her own, and I'm not going to sit by idly while not doing anything. Her parents have always liked me, especially her father, so I know he'll surely back me up when I offer the help. They had a few farmhands to pitch in during the busy season since Winter and her siblings moved away, but I haven't seen them around this year since I've been home. I'm guessing either they moved away, or things could possibly be a little tighter around the farm this year with Winter's dad being hurt.

She hangs up from her call with a sniffle. She manages to keep her tears at bay now, but I wish we were somewhere more private so she wouldn't attempt to put on a brave façade right now. "They opened up an investigation. They cancelled my card and are sending me a new one to my parents' house. A lot of good that'll do me right now, though, with the negative sign haunting me."

"Hey, it's the first step. Take a deep breath and try to visualize it all working out. Then say it out loud so I can hear you. Put the positive energy out into the world by speaking it into existence."

Her head tilts. "What kind of Voodoo Zen sort of stuff have you been into the past several years?" She asks, and I can't help but smirk. With my lip tipping up in response, she complies, inhaling deeply, then exhaling slowly. "The bank is taking the first step, and this is all going to work out. I'll find a way to handle everything, I always do."

My brow is furrowed when she opens her eyes, the deep sienna sparkling depths trained on me once again. What does she mean by she always finds a way to handle things? What else has she had to deal with since we've both gone our separate ways? And why does the thought of her dealing with anything alone bother me so badly?

I stand suddenly, my chair scraping against the floor as I shuffle to my feet. My hands clench and then release as my emotions begin to bubble up inside of me. She's already upset, and she doesn't need to deal with any sort of vibe coming from me right now. I can't allow my feelings for her to get in the way of the problems she's facing; she doesn't deserve the added pressure. "I have to go. Coach expects us to practice hard today since we'll be off our restrictive diets tomorrow."

"Ah, yes. For a moment there, I almost thought you were normal and forgot that you're actually a famous hockey star. I'm sure my problems are the last thing you want to deal with today, and now I've ruined your jacket in the process. I hope you won't be too cold on your way to practice." She stands as well, the table between us acting as an island. Her walls are slamming back up, and I hate every moment of it.

"You know it's not like that. I'll be by tomorrow. Let me know if you need anything."

She turns away, but I'm not finished.

I grab her wrist, commanding her attention as I say, "And Winter? I mean it. Don't stress yourself over something that I can grab on the way over or whatever. I have my truck; it's no big deal."

She nods, and I wince, suddenly feeling like an even bigger jerk. I just unintentionally reminded her that her car's still stuck on the side of the road. So much for not bringing the mood down any lower.

"Thanks, I'll be sure to let you know." With her hands full of both of her cappuccinos, I lead us to the door and hold it open for her to go out first. The next time we step foot in this coffee shop, it'll be loaded down with Christmas decorations, but for now, the fake amber fall leaves still adorn the homey feeling entrance as we leave. The sweet smells from the freshly baked goods escape around us, following us outside and down the two steps, making me hungry even though I already ate earlier.

The frosty chill in the air hits us instantly, and my muscles clench from the cold and my lack of a jacket. Thankfully, I have a spare in my closet at Mom's. Now let's hope the old thing still fits me. "I swear it got colder from the time we went inside."

"Right?" she agrees. "Brr." And now I'm wishing my jacket were dry for an entirely different reason, because I'd offer it to Winter in a heartbeat to help her stay warm. "See you tomorrow," she says and takes off down the sidewalk.

"You're walking home?" I ask, about to offer to drop her off instead.

She doesn't respond to my question, instead calling over her shoulder, "Bye, Sean Spruce."

And somehow, I know it's the answer to my unspoken offer. She wants to walk back to the farm, probably needing the time it'll take for her to go over everything in her head before she's back to her peppy self; she usually is around her parents. I admire her resilience; heck, I respect it a great deal, too. She has had stuff hitting her back-to-back, and it'd be enough to make a lesser person crumble, but not Winter. No, she's determined to figure it all out, and I bet she does it while singing Christmas carols the entire way home.

I get to my truck a few minutes later and open up the back door, checking for my ratchet straps. I have the heavy-duty kind that can hold a ton of weight, so they should do the trick. As I climb behind the wheel, I press the start button and the engine fires to life, the heat instantly blaring on to warm the cab. Once my Bluetooth connects from my cell, I hit the number for the local mechanic shop. There's only one of course, and it's now run by a guy I graduated with. His father had owned it previously, and supposedly, his grandfather even before that.

"Hey man," I greet as soon as he answers.

"Sean, good to hear from you. What's up?"

"If I tow a friend's car to the shop, can you put some snow chains on her tires for me? I don't have her keys, so her alarm may be going off when I pull up."

He chuckles. "Yeah, buddy, I can make that happen for you."

"Thanks, I appreciate it. I'll cover the cost, then maybe you can give her a call and ask her to pick it up? Or should I tow it to her place?"

He whistles lowly before saying, "Dang, you must have it pretty bad for this woman. I guess the real question is, whose car are you planning on towing to the shop?"

"Just a friend, but I can't stand the thought of anything possibly happening to her if she attempts to drive in this weather. She's too stubborn to take care of things herself, so I want her surprised."

"Yeah, okay. I can do that for you, no problem. Do you want her to know it was you who brought the car in and footed the bill? I can drop it off for you."

I think on it for a beat before saying, "No, let's just call me a secret Santa."

He laughs again. "You go it."

"Thank you, see you later." I hang up, mentally checking off the first thing on my own list. I may be surrounded by hyper-independent women around here, but it doesn't mean I can't quietly make sure they're taken care of in the process.

Next up, I really do have to get to the Blizzards' rink for some solo hockey practice. I have a game after Thanksgiving, and I need to be ready. After practice, I'll work on getting Winter's car out of the snow pile and slowly tow it into town. Tomorrow I'll get started on 'Operation Help Winter Get Through Christmas.' If we become good friends again during the process, even better.

I swear she gets more beautiful each time I see her, and while I may've bowed out before where she's concerned, it's not something I'm willing to do twice.

I'm used to winning, and if that includes gaining Winter in the end, there'll be no stopping me.

Chapter Seven

Winter

I'm adding the finishing touches to my hair when the Spruces arrive for Thanksgiving. I picked a festively plum-colored shift dress, along with a thin pair of sheer black tights with tiny velvet black dots all over them, and paired the look with a simple stack of understated silver bangles and my taupe booties. I also have on a long-chained silver necklace with the dark garnet stone pendant my mother gave me many years ago as a graduation gift. The stone is large, and the silver encasement has details all around, making it anything but understated, and I never take it off.

I lean in, glancing all over my face in the mirror, making sure the bits of makeup I put on earlier are still how I like them. I'm already pale, and the snow certainly won't help my cause any. My lashes are wispy, better defined by a few coats of my Lash Blast mascara. They've grown longer naturally, from the organic castor oil I've been brushing them with nightly. I added a bit of taupe and plum eye shadow to my lid but kept it very light, along with a bit of lip stain, and then gloss on top. I'm looking polished but not in an overly done-up sort of way. I learned long ago not to wear blush on Thanksgiving because with all the food and then cheering on the football game, as well as the heat from the kitchen, I'll be red enough as it is. Another curse of not having any sort of tan going for me right now.

Anyhow, I'm determined not to look like a complete hot mess this time around when Sean sees me again. I'd like it for once if I were the one with the upper hand and not falling all over myself in his presence. While I won't hold my breath on that front, I'm hoping he'll at least not see me and instantly think I'm a charity case who can't get her life right.

On my way down the hallway, I pop into my parents' bathroom, swiping a spritz of Mom's perfume. It's some sort of essential oil blend a lady from the next town over makes for her. Whatever it is, it has mint, coconut, and vanilla in it, and I'm kind of obsessed, wearing it whenever I forget my usual. I attempt to quietly make my way down the hallway, wanting to get the chance to scope out Sean before he sees me. Yesterday at the coffee shop really meant a lot to me. He didn't have to be so kind and pay for my drinks after I spilled cappuccino all over him. Nor sit with me to make sure I was okay, let alone offer to help me with suggestions on what steps I should take.

I come to a stop, finding Sean and Calla just inside the doorway, removing their coats. I heard Mom and Dad greet them a moment ago, but now I quietly watch as they hang their coats on the designated hooks. Calla is beautiful as always in her own natural way. She has some dark bags under her eyes today, so she must've worked the night shift for a night or two this past week. The clinic where she and Mom work is small without a lot of staff, so if anyone needs to be admitted and they don't end up going to Noelville instead, then some of the staff have to stay at the clinic overnight with the patient. Both Calla and Mom love their jobs, but I've also heard about how it can be hard at times when they're being stretched too thinly.

Sean, however, appears to be in his prime. Even after a grueling practice on the ice, he claimed to have to attend yesterday, he somehow appears no worse for wear. His profession is a different story, though; those players can't afford to practice and work tired, or else they could seriously injure themselves.

Today he's wearing a hunter green sweater, the material thin enough so he doesn't overheat, but still somehow smooth enough that it looks super soft to touch. He's paired it with dark wash jeans that hug his thick thighs, making me wish I could get a peek from behind, too. The best part of the entire outfit is his tan *Hey Dude's* he's currently slipping off next to the door, revealing crisp white sock-clad feet. He had on a black leather jacket that he's already taken off, but I can easily imagine how amazing he looked in the full get-up when he first stepped inside.

"You can leave those on if you want," I say, giving up my spot, knowing if I stay and stare any longer, it'll be detrimental to my health in some way. I shouldn't want to look at this guy, nor be in the same room as he is, yet it seems this trip home, I'm destined to run into him around every corner. I didn't want to be nice to him, but after everything he's done for me since I've arrived, he doesn't deserve my cold shoulder. Now, if I can manage to keep my heart from hurting around him, or even worse, falling for his dashing self all over again, that's the real test of my willpower. I hate admitting it, that he sorta broke my heart all those years ago, and it's the real reason I was so upset about seeing him in the first place.

His brow jumps, eyes immediately finding me where I'm standing off to the side. "I left my boots at home so they wouldn't get your mom's floors muddy from the slush out there, but these managed to get some on them too." He replies, obviously thinking I'm calling out his choice of footwear when I wasn't trying to. He doesn't have to look like a lumberjack or a professional hockey player every time I see him; being casual is definitely okay in my book. In fact, I prefer it to always feeling underdressed and frazzled in his presence.

Calla's face lights up when she notices me. "Winter, how lovely to see you. My–oh–my, you look so beautiful today."

I grin in return. "Thanks, Mrs. Spruce, you look nice too. I love your belt," I compliment, meaning every word. She may be content spending her life in this village, but apparently, she knows all the good spots to order her accessories offline. "If you don't mind me asking, which site did you get it from? I need to check out their collections." Not that I have a mere penny left to my name to blow until the bank decides if they'll replace the money I was scammed out of, but a girl can still window shop.

"I got this at Sandies. I went in the other day looking for a few gifts, and she had several of these in stock. Other designs, too."

My brow jumps. That's new. Sandies didn't carry cute accessories like that the last time I was around visiting, or I would've been eager to check the store out once I got into town. I wonder what else she's started keeping in stock that I'd like. "I'll have to pop in then," I comment as she turns to Sean.

"Doesn't Winter look great in that dress, Sean? We need her to get one in your team's colors. I bet all of your teammates would be drooling over her if she wore it to a game. When do you play the Blizzards again?"

His posture stiffens, a frown turning his lips down immediately, but he doesn't comment on the sudden change in his demeanor. His serious stare meets mine again as he doesn't answer his mom's question. Instead, he compliments, "You look stunning."

Heat instantly fills my body all over, and I know it must be showing on my cheeks, too. My heart thumps a quick, excited beat in my chest for a moment from his attention. The tension's soon broken between us from Dad hobbling in on his crutches. He greets Calla first, then shakes hands with Sean. "Welcome, welcome! Mom and Dad will be around shortly. Glad you two could make it. Brenda's been in the kitchen since six a.m.."

Mom huffs, wiping her hands on a dishtowel she has tucked into the tie on her festive apron. She looks like a kitchen quarterback with it hanging there the way it does. "I like prepping early so I can watch the parade at the same time. After all these years, you already know this."

Plus, Mom doesn't want Gram coming in and overdoing it. She may be a feisty old lady, but she needs to take it easy at her age and not get too overwhelmed by helping Mom. She'll show up with Pop soon enough, her hands loaded with her prized desserts that she's won ribbons for at every fair and festival around she's entered in.

Dad flashes Mom a grin, then hobbles his way back to the kitchen. He has never been one to sit back in the past, while Mom prepared a feast for a small army each holiday. He's always been right there beside her, helping in any way he possibly could, so this must be driving him crazy not being able to meddle and get in the way. My siblings and I were the same way. I used to wake up early just to beat my brother and sister downstairs to have some alone bonding time with Mom while she taught me her secrets to the ultimate turkey dinner. The recipes she uses were passed down from Nan, on Mom's side. Gram, on Dad's side, can bake all the sweets, but the woman can't roast a bird to save her life.

"Mom, what do you need my help with?" At this rate, I'm looking forward to her keeping me busy for the first half of the day. I was dreading this day in general when I first heard Sean would be here, but after each problem I've been hit with since I arrived, Sean's no longer at the top of the list, and I'll happily take all the distractions I can get. If I even almost *think* of my debit card and my lost funds I'm waiting on, I tear up. I'm determined not to give myself the slightest chance of doing it today and worrying my family.

"Finish setting the table for me?" Mom suggests, and I instantly nod. I head for the dining room, already thinking about which napkin rings I'm going to use.

"You look good too," I admit later to Sean once our parents have dispersed. "Green is your color, but so is blue." I don't know why I open myself up to feeding him compliments, but the man is like a fresh cup of hot cocoa, and I can't seem to resist being suckered in.

He grins, shaking his head. "Don't let my coach hear you say that; he swears I was only made for green."

His main team color is hunter green, since they're the Pines, so I'm not surprised to hear as much. I want to tell him he was made for every color because he looks lickable in anything he has on, even a paper bag, but I refrain. These intrusive thoughts that hit me left and right whenever he's in my vicinity are rough, I swear.

"My lips are sealed." I offer with a smile, raking my gaze all over his impressive form, remembering the expanse of skin I saw at the coffee shop. I bet he's a beast with his shirt off.

His stare immediately falls to my mouth, pausing there long enough that I know it was the absolute wrong thing to say. We're keeping space between us, and I'm determined not to make it awkward today between us. I was all for avoiding him when he first told me about them coming for Thanksgiving, but after his sweetness he showed me yesterday that I can't stop obsessing over, I've silently called in a truce on my part where he's concerned.

"You didn't text me." He mutters, stepping into my space. I take one back, putting my back to the wall. He takes another step until we're nearly touching all over. One of his arms raises to rest on the wall above me, while his other hand moves under my chin. He applies just enough pressure so I tip my chin up, meeting his intense stare. I swear, if he leans in and kisses me right now, we can just put a fork in me, because I will be done for the day.

He's expecting a response, and I know he won't move until I give him one. Not that I want him to move at all, but if our moms come in and see us like this, questions will be asked. I eventually shrug, wondering if he can hear my heart thundering away the way I can from his proximity. "I didn't need anything."

"Mm. I wish you had given me some sort of task. I can handle making sure you're satisfied."

I swear I must have heard him wrong, because there's no way he just said what I think he did. He has a way with getting my jingle in a jam to the point I can't think when he's close enough to kiss. Or climb. *I'd happily do both.* I swallow before whispering, "I couldn't think of anything."

He shakes his head, with a click of his tongue, and something tells me he's thinking of putting me on his naughty list. Maybe my dream about that the other night holds some merit after all. I watch with rapt attention as he steps away and heads for the entryway. He reaches toward the narrow, tall table against the wall by the jackets, and I finally notice a large red and green cup from the Tasty Sip sitting there. In the next beat, he's back and holding the cup out to me.

"What's this?"

"Your favorite," he acknowledges, and I swear his cheeks seem a little pink with his admission.

My mouth drops open in pleasant surprise, "You brought me a *capp*?"

And is there an ulterior motive behind this? He doesn't strike me as the type to add salt to my drink or anything, but he does seem like he'd be one to use it to bargain or take a few sips. You know the 'quality control' excuse men like to use. Yep, I'm betting he's a taster, and the prospect of his lips being where mine will soon be should bother me more. Okay, simply put, it doesn't bother me at all, and that's a total red flag in operation: *Willpower Around My Ex*.

He nods, "Yep. With holiday spirit on top and all."

He remembered my sprinkles and mini marshmallows? Who is this man?

"Wow. This is nice, thank you. I can't believe you went in there on a holiday to surprise me."

He shrugs. "I'd go in every day, if you wanted me to."

My eyes widen, stunned that he just admitted that out loud. Don't get me wrong, Sean was always a sweet guy when we were younger, but he's taking it up a *big* notch for some reason. Especially, after all of my diabolical accidents I've had around him. Talk about embarrassing, and the sad part is, I haven't done anything worth mentioning to make karma my enemy right now.

"Noted, hockey boy, but you should be careful with words like that." I fire back, hooking my pinkie with his, and lead the way to the kitchen. It's bad enough that I already can't seem to peel my eyes off of him every time he's around, and the fact that I once carried a torch for the man. The last thing I need is even more reasons to fall head over heels for the guy.

He dutifully helps me set the table that's at its full length, the leaves added to comfortably accommodate everyone. I smooth the crisp mustard colored tablecloth, watching as the light streams through the dining room windows. The sun hitting it changes the color, making the tablecloth seem lighter than it actually is. The fabric is thick beneath my fingers, pressed to perfection before it was put away since the last time we used it. It was Nan's tablecloth from Mom's side, and it has these fanciful embroidered patterns she'd sewn on it herself. We only use it for special occasions like Thanksgiving. Mom has a few different colors that we also bring out to admire around the holidays.

"Where do you want this?" Sean asks a little while later.

He's holding the small, clear vase that's shaped like a bowl I used to hold the mixture of burnt orange and plum-colored chrysanthemums I put together yesterday afternoon. I added a few sprigs of greenery and finished it off by tying a bow around the middle of the bowl. With the snow outside, the blooms won't last long on Mom's porch, so I took advantage of having the fresh flowers to add some beauty to our Thanksgiving table setup.

"I should've made some decorative place cards," I comment, stepping back to admire our handiwork. Maybe some little pumpkins with our names or something to give it the extra touch. The warm glow from the tiny votive candles we placed near the ends of each side flickers warmly. "Are the candles too much?"

A snort comes from him, drawing my attention away from the special china and silverware we use for different occasions. His brows are raised, amusement dancing over his handsome features. "You're worried about not making place cards, and you think the candles are too much." He states.

My eyes turn to slits as I glare, annoyed that he had to point out the obvious of me being a bit over the top. It's weird enough not having my siblings around, and him doing this with me instead. He's obviously not used to me and my siblings trying to make it as fancy as we can to surprise Mom when she's ready to serve the food. We've done it since we were children; it all started the year my brother spent the week before fall break at school coloring everyone's placemats. It was game on from then, over who could add special touches to make each year a little different. Rather than tell him my life story, I spin on my heels and take off for the kitchen, ready for the next task.

Later, I'm outside huffing and puffing as I trek back and forth from the woodpile to the front porch. Mom said we're getting low on firewood, so of course I volunteered to grab some more. What a dumb idea, because it's cold outside and my cute *thin* Thanksgiving attire was not designed for this type of manual labor.

"Ouch! Shoot!" I drop the log I was carrying and check my hand. Sure enough, there's blood on it now.

"You okay?" A sudden looming presence at my side asks, making me jump in my cute heeled booties.

"Mmhm," I mumble, trying to ignore the way my body fires up with him beside me.

"Let me see," he demands, his much larger, warm hand takes mine, flipping it over to check out my palm. He leans in close, tilting my hand this way and that, and so help me, I get a whiff of his addictive cologne. If I pull away from him, I'll seem rude, but if I remain this close, I may just lean in and sniff his shirt.

"Uh, I'm okay. See, it's just a scratch." I attempt to step away, but he catches my wrist.

"It could be a nail. We may need to get your mom to look at it and give you a tetanus shot."

I roll my eyes, because really? This is not a big deal in the slightest, and he's the one overreacting now. Besides, I will fight him every step of the way if he thinks I'm missing Thanksgiving dinner with my family to get a shot over a scratch.

SAPPHIRE KNIGHT

Chapter Eight

SEAN

As soon as I'd stepped out on the porch looking for Winter, I'd heard her yelp. Her mom told me she was outside getting more firewood, so I came to see if she'd like me to take over for her or to at least help. I don't mind being out here; I'm used to the cold. I like it, even, I'd have to, or being a hockey player would be a hard pill to swallow since I'm always out on the ice.

Fire blazes in Winter's eyes, the only warning I get that she's about to argue with me. I can't help being concerned. When I heard her voice in pain, my entire body felt like it was ready to burst if I didn't get to her, and it wasn't in a good way. I leapt off the porch, ready to launch into a full sprint to find her, but luckily, she was right on the side of the house. I panicked at the thought of her being hurt, and it may not have been my finest moment to overreact, but I can't help it. With everything going on in her life right now, I'm feeling overly protective and worried about her. Or, at least that's what I silently tell myself to make my actions all seem rational.

"It's not a big deal, it's a scratch." She mutters again, while bending down and turning the log over a few times before standing back up. "See? No metal. Just a piece of wood that managed to cut me when I tripped." She shoots the wood a scowl, her irritation making me want to grin, but I hold it back. I know it'd only piss her off further, and I'm trying to keep the stress off her, not add more. She's like a little bear, cute and cuddly, but if you test her, she'll let you know in a heartbeat.

"You should have your mom look at it. I can finish getting the wood for inside."

"I'll help, I said I'm okay."

My brow furrows at her continuing to be stubborn. When she stares me down in protest, I decide I've finally had enough of her spice over this. I won't let her hurt herself anymore when I'm perfectly capable of handling the wood myself. She's apparently forgotten I've got a good foot on her and can take this in another direction, which I obviously am going to have to do with her fighting me on getting her beautiful butt back inside.

"Woman," it leaves me on a growl. Her mouth drops in surprise as red licks up her neck, and I know it's not from the chilly air. She's got a rosy nose already from that. "If you don't get that gorgeous behind back in the house and wash that cut to keep it from getting infected, I'm going to toss you over my shoulder and take you there myself."

A shocked squeak sound leaves her, then she's stomping off toward the front porch. It's the first time today I feel my lips pull into a wide smile. It's not every day I get to knock Winter off kilter, and I intend to enjoy every moment of it. It's only fair since each time I'm around her, I feel like I'm in a daze with butterflies swarming around inside my stomach.

The next time we're in the same room together is when we've all sat down for turkey dinner. The house smells absolutely heavenly, with all the food that's been prepared, along with a few small candles burning. I'd bet they're the same candles Winter made from last year's festival that Mom gushed over repeatedly. I had back-to-back games, so I was too busy traveling with the team and couldn't make it home. Mom was quick to fill me in on everything I missed, and I ended up flying her to my place for a couple of days. She stayed with me for Christmas Eve, Christmas, and the day after, but then it was back to work for me. The team got lucky this year with a lighter schedule right around the holidays, though I doubt it'll be the case next year as well.

Winter fidgets beside me once we're finished saying grace, drawing my attention to her once more. It took everything in me earlier not to lean in and kiss her when she was against the wall. She's never looked more enticing than in that moment, but I somehow managed to refrain. Then there was the incident outside with her huffing and puffing over me, telling her to come back inside, and Lord help me, but I wanted to toss her over my shoulder and show her just how strong and capable I truly am. One of these days, I'm not going to have enough willpower to stop myself from leaning in and tasting the gloss she has on her lips. I have a feeling that'll be the same day my life changes for good, because there's no way I'd ever be able to give her up again.

"How's the cut?" I ask right off the bat, hoping she had the sense to show it to her mom.

She grabs the mashed potatoes, plopping down a large dollop with more force than necessary while shooting me a half-glower. I'm guessing she hasn't mentioned it, and now that she's been called out, she's silently telling me to keep my mouth shut. Too bad for her, because there's no such luck. Nope, I fully intend on taking advantage of this dinner with her parents and grandparents present. For starters, I don't want the old man thinking he can scare me away from Winter like he did the last time. I was determined not to take anything from her future, but that time's over now. She's had her chance at going to college and doing whatever else she may've wanted to experience young. Now, however, she's fair game as far as I'm concerned.

"Fine, thanks for asking. It was nothing serious, *like I said*." She grumbles, passing me the bowl of potatoes. I add some to my plate as her mother zeroes in on her.

"What cut?"

Winter holds her palm up, and I notice two neat little butterfly bandages helping hold the now clean cut together. "I took care of it."

Her mom beams, "You did a good job."

I use it as an in to my original plan from the coffee shop. "I guess this means you'll need my help even more, now. I'm so glad I have more time off this season to help out. We'll figure out all the festival stuff we need to do together, Winter. Don't worry, I'll keep my word and help." I say, offering her a tender glance, then flash a happy smile around the table.

Her parents and my mother instantly seem intrigued. Her grandmother smirks, a twinkle shining in her gaze. Her grandfather, however, furrows his brow as his lips turn down. I don't know why this guy doesn't seem to be my biggest fan, but something has to give. I literally did what he asked me to; should I have done the opposite? Been stubborn and selfish and demanded he stay out of mine and Winter's business so she'd follow me to college like I'd originally hoped she would?

We've passed all of that now. We're adults with careers and homes, so there shouldn't be an issue with me courting his granddaughter.

"What are you talking about?" She practically hisses, her hand in front of her mouth as if the entire table can't hear her.

Just an FYI, we can all clearly hear her.

My gaze finds hers, and it takes all the strength I can muster not to get lost in her eyes and let her have her way with this. She's stressed enough, so I'm going to help her as much as I can. Even if I have to resort to using her family for help. "You know. Our discussion we had yesterday at the coffee shop."

Her eyes flare in panic, and I don't miss her hands clenching under the table. She probably wants to pile drive me to the ground right about now, but this is a family holiday, so I'm safe. Rotten of me to use it to my advantage? Probably, but who can blame a guy for finding an 'in' with *the one who got away*?

"You were saying how you're getting a late start on the Noel Falls Christmas festival, and I promised I'd help with everything when I'm in town. Remember?"

She releases a tense breath, her shoulders dropping a bit. Did she think I was going to mention the money issues with her account? I promised her I wouldn't, and despite what she may be thinking right now, I keep my promises.

"Oh, right. Uh, I'm sure you're busy. It's fine, I've got it." She responds with a glance around the table and a fake smile, covering up her brief moment of panic from before.

"I don't mind, truly. I'll help with whatever you need me to here on the farm, and also with the festival. Even putting the lights up on the porch or wherever, just like we already discussed during our coffee date." I'm stretching the truth by a lot, but it is what it is at this point. Surely fibbing a little doesn't count against me when it's for a good cause to help someone who needs it, right?

Her father, David, perks up. "Honey, you didn't tell us you'd had a coffee date and found someone to help." He trains his attention on me next, "Thanks, Sean. We all appreciate your help around here, seriously. I was worried Winter would have her hands full with everything, so this is a relief."

Brenda nods along, "Yep, just the farm animals alone can be overwhelming. It's a good thing you're going to be helping her out." She beams, and I don't miss the grumbling from the feisty woman beside me.

Gram Verna claps with delight. "And, now she'll have someone to help her prepare all the special homemade farm creations we've been making in our family for years. We've been long overdue to add a new person to the bunch."

Pop Frank sputters a bit at his wife's words, "Now, hold on a minute. You want to share our family recipes? But then they won't be the family's."

Gram Verna slugs him in the arm, "Hush up, you old fool. Sean Spruce is a pillar of the community. If there's any young man we can trust around here, it's certainly him."

Mom is watching everything play out and seems more than pleased with Verna's claim. "I think it's a wonderful idea, Sean. And Winter, if there's anything I can do on my days off as well, don't hesitate to ask. I may not know how to make candy or candles, but I can pick up supplies or anything else you may need. I know how to tie bows, too, if you want them to decorate your packages and the gift baskets."

Brenda reaches over, squeezing Mom's hand. "Thank you, Calla. You've done so much for our family already during this time. I hope you know how grateful we all are."

"You were there for me when Sean's father passed. It's the least I can do. You're not only my boss at the clinic, but you're family."

They both sniffle a bit, and I'm ready to shift this conversation in a happier direction. One where I now have a viable excuse to spend as much time around Winter as possible. Like I said before, when I play, it's to win, and she has no idea what I'm willing to do when it comes to her.

"Great, I have practice at the Blizzards' rink, and a couple of games, otherwise, I'll be here." I can't wipe the grin off my face as I stuff a bite of turkey and stuffing in my mouth, then chew. I hope Winter's ready to spend some time together, because I plan to be over here enough to the point, she no longer knows what her life is like without me in it.

Gram Verna takes a dainty bite of her green bean casserole and then asks, "So Sean, you never found a woman?"

I nearly choke on my roll. Coughing, I clear my throat. "Um, no, I've dated here and there."

"But none of those floozies stuck with you like Winter has?"

"Uh..."

"Gram!" Winter gasps, mouth falling open. She starts tossing out hand signals, but I miss them for the most part as I meet her grandmother's inquisitive stare. I'm not trying to be rude; I have a feeling this old woman could be my biggest ally when it comes to her granddaughter.

"Mom," David interrupts. "Let's not put Sean on the spot, the poor guy. These two have managed to stay friends, and I wasn't so sure after Winter cried nonstop for nearly a month straight after he left to play college hockey. Let's just be thankful they've pushed past any previous animosity."

Frank nods, "It's turkey dinner. Let's discuss football."

Winter's pale as a ghost, seemingly mortified as she glances between her father and grandmother, vigorously shaking her head at them both.

"Actually," I peer over at the stunning woman by my side, wanting her to know where I stand, so she doesn't have any misconceptions about my feelings, past or present. I wasn't planning on saying anything about this right now, but I may as well, so not only does she know, but so does the entire table. "None of them ever held a candle to your granddaughter, and that was all the confirmation I needed to know that they were never the one for me."

***

I'm in Canada, having just played our last game for the week, when I finish telling Jake, my best friend and teammate, what happened at Thanksgiving. I'm met with stark silence, not used to him *not* having an opinion on something. His mouth opens and closes a few times before he finally responds. "You told her how you feel in front of her family? They all heard you say it?"

I nod, aware that everyone else, for the most part, is eavesdropping on our conversation. I'm sure a couple of them are fighting themselves from commenting.

"Dude. You're brave, I'll give you that, but also crazy, my friend. What if her father flipped out and threw the potatoes at you or something?"

I stop unlacing my skate to glance up at him. He's completely serious. "Jake, what kind of people are you having turkey dinner with that are okay with throwing the bowl of potatoes?" That's literally never happened at any of the holiday dinners I've been to, and we've gone to several different houses for the occasion.

His hands go up, staring at me like I'm the crazy one for asking. "I have sisters, okay? Trust me when I say things get heated when you're the only guy in a house with four sisters and a mom who still thinks she's thirty. You should've seen the time one of them showed up with a dude my mom dated. We didn't get to eat anything that day because it was all over the dining room walls. I'm more concerned that it never crossed your mind that something similar could've happened at Winter's house when you went all *book-boyfriend* on her. Does she know about how you towed her car to the mechanic shop yet?"

"Book boyfriend? What does that even mean? And no, she hasn't figured out yet that I've done anything with her car. Besides, I told them to make sure she thinks it was a Secret Santa who had her car towed."

He snorts, shaking his head. "Yeah, you pulled something straight out of one of my sister's romance novels. Going all open heart at dinner and then fixing her car without her knowing." He chuckles, yanking the tape off the top of his skates.

I shift my pants down, finally out of my skates. I'm a sweaty mess; I played my butt off tonight and am ready for a hot shower to scrub the grit off. "And you know what your sister's books are like, because…?"

He rolls his eyes with a huff, "All I'm saying is, don't knock the books until you've read a couple. You'd learn some things, man, trust me."

I shake my head, double-checking the guards on my skates before setting them in my large duffel bag. I grab my travel towel and some fresh clothes, then quickly hit the shower. Thankfully, this arena is huge, so the locker rooms are more on the posh side than some of the others I've been to. Jake returns from the showers at nearly the same time I do, so we pick up the conversation where it left off.

"What did she say when she found out you've been carrying a candle for her all these years? Are you finally back together? I mean, she's always been the one that got away, right?"

"Nah, we're not back together. The subject got changed. Her grandfather isn't my biggest fan, so he turned the convo to football. Then, before I got another chance to talk about it with her, she was out taking care of the animals on her parents' farm. Mom and I ended up leaving not long after, since she had to work at the clinic first thing in the morning and I had to fly out for our games."

Chris Christianson, another of my teammates who's been listening in the entire time, shoulders into our space, "Bro, not good.

You shouldn't have left without *something* from her. Even if she said something along the lines of she needed time to think or whatever, you don't want to leave it all in the dark."

A groan of frustration escapes as I run my hand through my damp hair and then use the towel to dry it off some more. Thankfully, I don't have to rush out of here still dripping wet, since it's not my night to worry about media time. "I was trying not to force it and smother her. I'd been around her all day, making myself useful to her whenever I could, so I figured at that point I'd be coming on too strong. You've heard of the *'ick,'* right? Chicks get it for random stuff, and I didn't want to force my feelings on her, because if she gets the ick, then I'm completely done for."

"Crash and burn, Spruce," my teammate, Randy Stocking, admonishes, now deciding he's a part of this private conversation as well. He peers over at me while putting on his deodorant, like I'm the team's last hope and just blew it. On the contrary, I scored the winning goal earlier, thank you very much. I may not have everything figured out with Winter to fit into a neat little box, but even I know that potential relationships don't work that way.

I sigh, asking, "All right, what would you guys have done if you were in my shoes, then?" They think they know everything, so let's hear this grand master plan they'd have implemented in my place.

Chris speaks up first, while busily tying his shoe. "Well, for starters, I wouldn't have let her go outside to take care of the animals alone."

Randy nods, tossing a chip in his mouth. He chews and swallows, then agrees. "Yeah, for sure. You should've taken advantage of the alone time." He tosses the chips back on the shelf and slides his arms into his blazer.

Jake agrees, sliding his team hoodie over his head. He rights it and comments, "Yep. And if it were me, I would've kissed her. Laid a big one on her so she felt it all the way down to her toes. Then, at least you'd know if the spark is still there after all these years."

"The spark is still there," I confirm immediately, my irritation growing at even the mere thought of losing my connection with her from before. "I don't need a kiss to know. I don't need *anything*; just seeing her face again after so many years was enough to know. And guys? It's not a spark when it comes to her, it's a lightning bolt slamming straight into my heart."

Whistles and cheers with a bit of razzing ring out around me, and I can't help but chuckle, shaking my head. One day, they'll get hit with it, too, and then they'll know exactly what I mean when I say there's only ever been *one* woman.

CHAPTER NINE

WINTER

    His words have been playing on repeat in my mind ever since they left his mouth. That was a week ago, FYI. He's been traveling all over the country for his games, so I've had nothing but time in his absence to think.

    Talk about taking a hit from the left, I never imagined those words would tumble free from his lips, let alone at the dinner table during Thanksgiving in front of my family. I may've fantasized about him saying them a time or two over the years, but I'll never be caught admitting as much. And now, it's only a matter of time before my siblings find out, and I'm bombarded by them with questions that I don't have the answers to. I'm surprised my phone isn't ringing already from one of them having heard the news from Mom or Gram, but maybe I have the poor cell service to thank for it. It'll only be a matter of time before they try the landline.

Thankfully, I haven't had to see Sean since the big reveal. It had me in a chokehold all the way until dinner ended, and I was able to escape outside to care for the animals. I'm beginning to wonder if the distance wouldn't be by his choice after everything, but only because he's been working. Me, on the other hand, I have needed the space desperately to think and attempt to get my head back in the game. I don't want to simply fall at Sean's feet, asking for another chance.

Dad was adamant about turning his game on the other night, and I have a feeling he'll do the same thing tonight, too, so I haven't been completely free of the gorgeous hockey player. I couldn't stop myself from watching, even though I tried. In the end, I was glad I didn't miss the entire game, because I got to see Sean score a goal.

Then there's Gram. I swear the gleam in her eyes has only gotten brighter with each day, as she casually mentions Sean in some way. Something tells me the sparkle isn't from the newest snowfall we received last night, and she's silently plotting. I guess she could be in the eggnog again, but at this point, I'm not putting anything past her and plan to keep my eye on her.

I finish feeding the chickens and collecting their eggs in a basket, then make my way toward the house. I drop the basket off next to the front door so I don't forget to take them inside once I'm finished out here and head to the barn. I grab the first bin I find inside and trek back to the porch again. It has Christmas decorations written on it, so I'm sure we'll need it. Mom was determined to decorate the day after Thanksgiving like we do every year; however, she hasn't had the chance to be home much. A couple of new patients turned up at the clinic who needed to be admitted and monitored, so she's been busy caring for them.

The bank finally got a hold of me this morning with an update. Thankfully, the phone rang in one of the few spots we have cell service at on the farm, and I was able to take their call. I'd been worried it wouldn't be the case, and I'd end up overdrawn for the foreseeable future. Anyhow, they decided in my favor and refunded the money I was scammed out of. On the downside, I'm still waiting to get my new card in the mail. It's okay, though, at least I have the money in my account now to pay my rent that's overdue. It's an automatic draft, so I don't need my card, luckily. Since their call and the reassurance from their fraud department, it's felt like a huge weight has been lifted off my shoulders.

Now, I need to drink plenty of cappuccinos this week to have lots of energy to get everything in order for the festival. I'll start on the honey body butter first, since it stays the freshest longest, and the scent only gets richer with time. It's one reason why I've always made it in November in the past, so the essential oils would have extra time to work their magic for the holidays.

"Hi, Winter!" Calla calls, surprising me.

I was so caught up in my thoughts that I didn't notice her vehicle parked in the driveway. Her breath puffs around her, and I can see the white mist from my spot as she steps off the porch. It must've dropped a few more degrees since I went into the barn, which means we'll probably be getting another round of snow tonight. I need to check the forecast, because at this rate, I won't get my car back until the spring. If that happens, my boss will not be amused at me attempting to work remotely with a temperamental internet service. I wouldn't be surprised if my car is a solid chunk of ice from being parked on the side of the road, but it's not something I can worry about right this minute.

Speaking of ice, the path to Gram and Pop's place needs to be shoveled and salted. That's one job I'll gladly offer Sean if he shows up willing to help anytime soon. The last thing I want to do is shovel snow, and my to-do list just keeps piling up higher and higher. I wonder if Dad's heated blower is fixed, so I can try to use it instead. The walk from house to house isn't far, but it's enough to have your back screaming for a solid week if you try to handle the shoveling all at once.

"Hi Calla, is everything okay?"

She nods. "Your mom asked me to drop by with some groceries."

"Thank you. I wish she'd have said something because I would've gone." Dad's old fifties pick up will make it to the market and back, no problem. I'd have to wrap myself in a blanket since the heat doesn't work too great, but that's beside the point.

She waves me off, walking to her car. "I was headed there anyhow. Sean is supposed to be back tomorrow; he has two days off before his next game. Did you catch the last?"

"Yeah, uh, Dad turned it on. He played great."

She beams. "He'll be so happy to hear you were watching and saw him score! I'll be sure to tell him you were watching when he calls tonight. Bye, Winter." She opens her car door to climb inside.

"Wait, that's not what I meant!" I sputter, but it's too late. She's already tucked inside her vehicle, putting her seatbelt on. A beat later, she's turned her car around and is driving back down the long driveway.

"Ahhh!" I scream into the quietness, once her car has disappeared completely from view. With a heavy exhale, I set another bin of decorations on the edge of the porch.

The front door opens, and Dad pokes his head out with his brow furrowed. "Hey, everything okay out here? I thought I heard screaming?"

Just great.

I swear I'm losing my mind on this trip. My family will think I'm losing it, too, if they hear me randomly screaming outside, but I couldn't help it. Sometimes you have so much scrambling going on in your mind that the best thing to do is to pause and yell with all of your might.

"I thought I found something, turned out to be nothing," I reply with the straightest face I can muster.

He stares at me for a beat, and I can tell he's not buying it one bit. He's been around women long enough not to call me out on it, but rather, just nods. "Okay, then. Calla brought some of the fresh tomato basil soup we like from the sandwich shop with the groceries, if you're hungry."

We've been on a Thanksgiving dinner leftover kick the past few days, so soup without turkey floating in it is a nice change. I had pecan pie and whipped cream for breakfast today. I figure if I'm being forced to eat nothing but leftovers, the pie will be mine. Bedside's pecan pie is practically the same thing as honey and granola, so it still counts as breakfast food.

I nod. "Thanks, I'm going to grab a few more bins, then I'll be in."

We're interrupted by a truck coming up the driveway, its headlights shining brightly as the vehicle gets closer. It's that weird sort of winter day, where it almost seems gray outside from the low-hanging snow clouds that hide the sun and light away. Yet, it's bright all in the same way, from the expanse of white snow covering nearly everything.

I peer over at Dad for a second, waiting for him to go back inside. When he doesn't budge, I eventually ask, "You expecting anybody?"

"Nope. And it's too snowy on the mountain with the fresh powder for us to get any extra deliveries right now." He finally hobbles out from where he'd been perched in the front doorway and ventures further onto the porch. He holds the column so he can lean over and see the truck approaching for himself. After a beat, he mutters, "Looks like Doug Henderson from the shop in town."

"Wait, the same Doug I went to school with?" He was a grade higher, but I still saw him almost daily for most of my life. This place is small after all, and you'd have to be homeschooled in order not to know someone. Even then, it'd still be strange because the community is close-knit.

"Yep, the same one," he confirms as the vehicle finally pulls up to the house. It's not just any truck, either; it's a big, beefy tow truck.

With my car hooked on the back!

Doug hops out, giving a respectful nod to Dad, and then grins my way. "Hey, Winter. I heard you were back in town for the holidays. Welcome home."

I forgo all appropriate greetings and instead opt for, "Doug, you got my car for me?"

My eyes are the size of saucers as I watch, with my mouth slightly ajar in surprise. He rounds the truck and begins messing with stuff. His big clunky snow boots leave a trail behind him that I want to follow while asking a million questions, but I manage to remain rooted in my spot, transfixed. I'm not an excited puppy or anything of the sort, no matter how overjoyed seeing my car in my parents' driveway makes me feel inside.

"This is the nicest thing anyone's ever done for me. Seriously. I was just worrying over my car earlier, hoping no one would hit it while out snowplowing in the dark."

He shakes his head, "I wish I could take credit for this, but it wasn't me. A secret Santa brought it to my shop a few days ago. Pulled it in himself with his truck. He must've been going ten miles an hour the entire way to make it happen. I'd have had it to you sooner, but he insisted I order you some new tires and put some chains on for you. I thought I had everything in stock, but he kept calling and adding things for me to do, so I didn't. I was finally able to get all the parts in yesterday before the snow hit again."

"A secret Santa?" I mumble to myself, as Dad's curious stare pings between me and our unexpected delivery.

Doug continues," Anyhow, the car is good to go now. Stick to running errands while the snow is deep. You know how it is, no tire and chain can prevent a serious accident if the ice is bad enough, that's all on Mother Nature. And just so we're clear, I didn't tell you who your secret Santa is."

"Who is it?" My chin raises with the question. My hands land on my hips as I ready myself to wear him down into a confession if needed.

"Sean. But like I said, I'm Ft. Knox over here." He mimes zipping his lips shut, and I nod, still promising nothing but giving the illusion I'm as secretive as an elf on double list duty.

Dad whistles lowly, pulling my attention back to the porch. His brows are sky high, nearly in his hairline, as he shoots me a pleased look. I don't need him to say anything out loud; I can read the approval written all over him from a mile away while he proudly wears his fluffy Santa hat. Everything about his expression conveys that Sean Spruce is a top-notch provider in his book. He's basically on marriage-level at the moment, with taking care of his daughter by making sure I have my car and can safely drive it. I refrain from rolling my eyes, but it's not easy. I'm on to Dad and his not-so-subtle nudge in the hockey player's direction.

Doug gets my car lowered to the ground and unhooked, then puts the rest of his equipment away before he stops in front of me. He holds his hand out, my key dangling in front of my face, "Here you go. I changed the oil, filters, and topped you up on your fluids. You'll probably need a new belt or two soon. Nothing wrong with them, they've just been known to go over time with the weather and wear and tear. If you're in town when they snap, give me a call and I'll have it fixed in a jiff. Sean put a credit on file for you in case the car needs any work done."

I'm stunned speechless, and a lack of words is typically not something I'm used to having an issue with. I can't believe that crazy man did all of this for me, and I had no idea. I take the key, offering a wobbly smile while noticing he has a bit of grease smudged on his cheek now. It's endearing, so instead of letting him know, I keep it to myself. Not very Christmassy of me, but I'm sure some lonely woman in town will appreciate the *'in'* I've just given her.

"We appreciate your help, young man. Whether Sean paid you for it or not," Dad calls, his face pink from the cold and standing on the porch without his jacket this entire time. He's practically beaming from ear to ear after hearing Doug's spiel on everything he's fixed.

I nod. "Um, he's right. Thanks, Doug. I appreciate you doing all of that car stuff you mentioned, truly. I honestly thought I probably wasn't going to have a vehicle until spring at this rate, so it's a great surprise."

He grins. "I'm glad. Okay, I'm out of here. See you at the festival and Merry Christmas!"

"See you there," I respond, wearing a smile. It hits me right then that he's just given me my car key. The same key I had inside with me this entire time. Or so I thought. "Wait, how did you get my car key?"

He pauses for a second before stepping up onto the side step of his truck. "Sean brought it to me Thursday night. He mentioned he'd just had dinner over here with you all and was taking his mom home. Have a good one." He calls, then he ducks inside his tow truck and carefully turns the oversized vehicle around to drive away.

Oh, that sneaky, sneaky nutcracker! Sean was plotting the entire time!

I knew the Thanksgiving cappuccino he'd brought to butter me up with had ulterior motives behind it. He must've grabbed my car key when he hung up his jacket, and I never had the slightest clue. How could I when he so easily distracted me the entire day?

He showed up with my favorite drink, going so far as to remember the whipped cream and holiday cheer on top. Then, he flirted in his own Sean sort of way, and nearly kissed me when we were supposed to be setting the table. Later, he came outside all growly and bossy, which did nothing but stoke the flames to my libido, making me want him even more, just to end up having a dinner I'll never be able to forget. It looks like I never stood a chance against his plans, and for some reason, it only makes me want to challenge him further.

Dad goes back in the house now that the excitement is over, taking the basket of fresh eggs with him, leaving me in comfortable silence. I pull out my cell, glancing at the screen. I know I should at least text Sean and tell him thank you, but my nerves right now are getting the best of me.

With a huff, I stuff my phone back in my coat pocket and head for my car. I glance through the driver's side window as I hit the unlock button, only to find a small wrapped gift box on the dashboard. Of course, it spurs me on to hurry up and hop inside. There's no tag or anything, just a small box wrapped in hunter green paper with lighter green trees and white snowdrops all over it. It's finished off with a thin white ribbon tied into a bow. My stomach flips with excitement over the unexpected present. Nothing says I can't open it right now, so I carefully pull the ribbon and tear open the paper. I open the box and peer inside.

Tucked amongst some tissue paper is a keychain. It has a silver 'W' that has my birthstone gem on each peak of the letter; there's a snowflake hanging on one side, and on the opposite side is an angel. I turn it over, noticing script on the back of her dress.

May this angel watch over you and keep you safe. Travel slowly, so her wings can keep up.

I softly rub my thumb over the words, feeling my heart thawing a touch toward the gorgeous, thoughtful jock. He wants her to keep me safe. It's seriously the sweetest thing. Something so small can suddenly mean so much, and make the fact he'd swiped my car key in the first place disappear.

I replace my old keychain with the new key ring Sean got me, then tuck it safely in my coat pocket and get out of my car. With an unsteady exhale, I stride toward the barn. I have lots of bins to get out, and right now, I'll take any distraction I possibly can from thinking about the hot hockey player and how hard he's making it for me not to fall for him.

SAPPHIRE KNIGHT

CHAPTER TEN

SEAN

Thankfully, the red-eye flight after my last game was quick, and I was able to get back to Noel Falls without any issues. There was more snow on the ground when I arrived than when I left a week ago. Luckily, I had my truck at the airport, so I took it slow on the mountain.

Mom was there to greet me as I walked through the door of my family home, waiting to tell me how proud she was of my playing. While I appreciate her compliments, my playing well still wasn't enough to clinch the win for our last game. We won our first game, only to turn around and bomb the next with the Leafs. For some reason, our line wasn't gelling together like we usually do, and when Coach started switching us out, it only went downhill from there. Royce, our Captain, attempted to pull us together, but even he didn't possess the magic touch we needed at the time to make a solid comeback. Anyhow, I crashed as soon as my head hit the pillow after such a long day.

When I woke up today, however, thoughts of the game were no longer at the front of my mind. The only thing I seem to be able to think about at all is seeing Winter. The aches and pains that come from playing such a brutal sport back-to-back can't even keep me away, so I sat in Mom's oversized tub with some ice. Teeth-clenching and all, I waited until my body was numb enough that I could make it outside to the hot tub. After twenty minutes or so of soaking out there, my patience ran thin, and in the next blink, I was dressed and hurrying out the front door.

I pull up to the farm, my stomach already swirling with anticipation of seeing her. As soon as I shift the truck into park, I open my door, hit the ignition button, and jump out. I grab the two cups I got from Tasty Sip before closing my door. Her car is parked next to mine in the driveway, and I'm glad to see it was already delivered. Hopefully, she won't be too pissed off over me having the new tires put on without her permission. I'm sure she'll demand to pay me back, or else be furious that I took it upon myself to make decisions without asking her first, but we'll deal with that when it comes time. I know one person who'll appreciate me looking out for his daughter, and aside from Winter, I have a feeling David's who I need to impress around here the most.

I quickly take the three porch steps, noticing the rich green garland and deep red bows wrapping around the porch pillars as well as framing the front windows and door. A throw and festive pillows are arranged neatly on the porch swing at the end, with various lanterns, poinsettias, tall candles, large gold bells, and a sled painted with the words: *'Wishing All A Merry Christmas,'* decorate the rest of the space.

Not only that, but there's so much mistletoe, you'd think this was a kissing booth.

It looks like someone has been keeping busy since the last time I was here. I know it wasn't her mom because mine told me all about how distracted they've been at the clinic with new patients pouring in each day. I can't help but smile as I take in the rug at the front door. It has *'No Naughty Elves Allowed,'* painted in deep black, a contrast to all the red, green, white, and gold adorning the other decorations.

I raise my hand, but before I have the chance to knock, the door is pulled open. David stands there, his good arm braced on the door frame to keep him from wobbling. "I thought I heard a vehicle." He mutters as I meet his kind eyes.

"Expecting a delivery?"

He shakes his head and chuckles. "Nope, but I was curious if you'd have any more cars dropped off. Want to fix my wife's SUV or my truck next?" He offers, while a grin tugs at the corner of his mouth, and I laugh. "Got a tractor or two around here as well that needs a bit of TLC."

My hand comes up to rub at the back of my neck as I smile and admit, "I didn't think it'd be a good idea to leave her car on the side of the road. Then, at Thanksgiving, when I learned your tractor doesn't have any heat, I was glad I took care of it. Knowing Winter, she'd be stubborn enough to try and drive the tractor to tow her car home, and end up with hypothermia."

David nods, pulling a bite-sized pecan pie he had stashed from his breast pocket, and eats half of it. He chews for a moment before agreeing, "Mmhm. You're right about that one. I appreciate you taking care of it for her. She'll need that, you know?" He sticks the other half of the mini pie back in his T-shirt pocket, distracting me.

My brow furrows as I silently wonder if he'll remember the snack later or if it'll end up in the washer. Should I say something about it?

"She'll need that, you know?" he repeats, and I meet his stare, finding him smirking.

With a relieved exhale, I relax a bit, knowing he's pleased with me helping. "Need what?"

"Someone who won't back down from her, who will step in to help her when she needs it. I don't know if you've noticed or not, but my daughter can be very independent and headstrong. She hasn't learned the importance of leaning on others yet, but I'm afraid that's something you only learn with time. I'll be honest, I wasn't too excited when you were kids and dating in high school. Not because of anything you did, on the contrary, I thought you were a decent kid. It was my Winter, I worried about. She needed room to grow into her own woman, whatever that was going to eventually look like."

"And now? Would it be okay if I hung out with her and possibly dated her? If she were open to it?"

He reaches out with his good arm, giving my shoulder a quick, firm squeeze. He replies, "I think you're just the right one to get close to her, Sean. Something tells me she'd push anyone else away, and this Christmas, I'd like to see my daughter happy and in love. She deserves to have someone to spend her time growing old with. So yeah, I'm okay with you dating my daughter. I'd even be okay if you wanted to marry her sometime, too."

Her father's approval means much more to me than I ever imagined. Maybe because Dad isn't here any longer, and David would be the closest person to another father figure I'd have in my life if Winter were to give me another chance. "Thank you, that means a lot. Is she here?"

He gestures toward the barn, "Been out there working all morning. Yesterday she fussed over the porch. Today, she was going to get the rest of the decorations pulled down from the barn shelves and then get herself organized on festival supplies to see what all she still needs. Is one of those for her?" He gestures at the two cups I'm still holding.

I nod. "Yeah, stopped on my way to get her favorite. I figure it may be best to approach her with caffeine and sugar after I've had her tires and stuff replaced."

He chuckles. "Smart man, and great job on the games. We were rooting for you over here."

"Thanks. I'm going to go find her before this cappuccino cools down, and she tosses it at me."

He's still laughing as he shuts the door, and then I'm striding toward the big red barn not far from the house. I carefully watch my steps since there's fresh snow on the ground, and I don't know where ice may be. I'm also a little sore from taking a rough hit in the last game, so I don't want to bust my butt in the process.

Some work around the farm with Winter over the next couple of days, and my regular practices at the Blizzards' rink in the next city over will do me a lot of good and help me shake off that last game. We're good this year, but even one loss can mess up a team and set the precedent for the rest of the season. I feel like I have an advantage since I'm able to practice while at home for the holidays. I get some outside perspective and time where I only concentrate on myself, instead of worrying about the team as a whole on the daily. Don't get me wrong, I love my team, and we work well together. However, it's getting a little more difficult to click with some of them as I'm the oldest on the ice whenever we practice together.

Music greets me as I get closer, effectively stealing me from my work thoughts. I open the barn door, peeking my head inside to make sure Winter's in here and hasn't disappeared to visit some of the animals. My eyes find her immediately, watching as she dances and sings along to the song playing. She's busily working in front of the long wooden counter her dad built many years back.

I still remember him coming in for the supplies and telling me all about it. I was sixteen at the time and working part-time at the local hardware store. I even had to do a delivery out here and drop off some supplies, and saw it in the making. I thought nothing of it at the time. I suppose the project probably made me think of my own father at the time, missing him, and somehow knowing he'd be doing the same stuff around our house if he were still alive. Seeing something David had built many years ago, still being put to good use and holding up, makes me think of my future with a family someday as well.

Will we have our own family business at some point, where we'll rush around to create something in time for the festival as well? I can't help but wonder what that future will look like when I finally have someone to share it with. Could Winter be the woman I create all those memories with? I know one thing: I certainly hope it's her. If the electricity I feel whenever I'm around her is anything to go by, I'd say she's the one and only for me, no matter how much time has passed.

Rather than be a creeper and watch her any longer, I stroll inside the big barn. Winter has a piping bag in one gloved hand while the other helps direct the fluffy stuff into clean glass containers. "How's it going in here?" I ask loud enough that she can hear me over the music.

"Ah!" She jumps and releases an adorable shriek. She's so cute, I swear. "Jesus, put a bell on!"

"Huh?" I chuckle, holding up one of the cups so she notices I've come with a peace offering.

"You move like a cat. You need to wear a bell or something so I hear you ahead of time."

I nod, wearing a smirk. I'm used to moving with a bit of grace on the ice when I'm not slamming into people and stealing pucks, so I get it. "A bell might be weird, but I'll see what I can do about being nosier for you. What are you doing?" I gesture behind her to the rows upon rows of glass jars she's filled perfectly to the point of leaving a small lip at the top. It's fluffy-looking stuff, reminding me of thick whipped cream.

"These are the sweet honey body whips. I've been making them since yesterday. I mixed it all yesterday and added in the different scents. Today, I'm putting it in the jars, and then some will be put into small boxes, while the others will be added to various gift baskets. Is that little burst of sweet hot heaven for me?" She nods to one of the cups I'm holding.

"I thought you might need a boost since you have a lot to accomplish." I hold out the one in my right hand, loving the smile she rewards me with in return. She eagerly takes the cup, and I can't stop myself from reaching forward, giving her hip a gentle squeeze. More than anything, I want to tug her to me, wrap my arms around her, and just hold her. I've missed her since I've been gone, and the happiness I'm feeling right now from being in her presence again doesn't escape me.

"Mm," she sips, her eyes closing as she savors the first drink.

I shouldn't be imagining her having that look for other reasons, but I can't help which direction my mind goes. The woman is smoking hot, and to witness her dancing around in a pair of tight leggings, shaking her booty, well, let's just say my mind definitely went there, and I can't get the image out of my mind.

"If you keep this up, I may become a little spoiled," she admits, gazing at me through her lashes.

"I'm counting on it," I disclose, and watch with rapt attention as her breath catches.

CHAPTER ELEVEN

SEAN

Her expression softens a touch as she stares at me for a beat before the trance is broken up by one of the horses nickering, and another snorting. The commercial currently on the holiday playlist she's been listening to ends, and then another carol begins to play.

"I'm guessing they're fans of the Christmas tunes?"

She nods, grinning. "Oh, absolutely. This is a Christmas farm in case you missed all the decorations. We've all got it bad, even the horses."

I shake my head, smiling like a fool. *A fool for her.* "How can I help? Put me to work, *Boss*."

"*Mm, boss.* Yeah, I like the sound of that. You can start by screwing the lids on each of these jars after I put the plastic protector thingy on."

"Plastic protector thingy, got it." I nod and step up beside her at the counter.

I'll admit I'm feeling a bit relieved she's not throwing the hot cappuccino at me and chasing me out of here for taking care of her car for her. If her dad knew it was me, then there's no way she hasn't figured it out as well. Doug probably caved and told her two minutes into the delivery that I was the one responsible. I know I should've asked her first about doing anything to the vehicle, and I would've, but I also know she's stubborn enough to have told me no. It's one of those situations where I decided it was better to act first and then apologize if needed, versus asking permission ahead of time.

"Dad had your games on. We saw them both. Are you okay after that hit yesterday?"

Mom already mentioned that Winter had said she watched my game, but I didn't think she'd pay close enough attention to catch the hit. It feels good knowing she saw me play and watched enough of the game to be comfortable asking questions.

"You like hockey?" I find myself asking instead of answering her right away.

She watched me play when we were younger, but the whole village showed up to my games, it seemed, whenever they had the chance. The community is probably a little too involved with school activities around here, but they find joy in it. The kids benefit the most from it in the end with all of the added support. Our bake sales were legendary back then, with all the older ladies wanting to pitch in.

"Of course, I like hockey. I like several sports, that hasn't changed over time. If anything, I enjoy them even more than when you used to know me."

"When I *used* to know you..." I repeat, trailing off, before moving forward. I don't like the idea of not knowing her for any amount of time we've been a part. I can't stop asking myself why I waited this long to see her again in the first place. I feel like I've wasted so much time we could've had together. I was an idiot to ever let this stunning woman out of my grasp. "I'm okay. The team doc checked me over and said no concussion, so I can still play."

"Your head may be okay, but what about the rest of you? I'm not worried if you can play; I'm concerned about whether you're injured." She pauses in her task, meeting my gaze, and I find true apprehension in hers. "You obviously didn't break anything because you still played in the game, but you must be sore?"

I decide to just be honest about it and lift my jacket, along with the layered thin shirts underneath it, so she can see for herself. "I had enough time to sit in an ice bath before my flight last night and then again this morning."

She draws in a swift, shocked gasp as her hands fly to her face, covering her mouth. Her eyes roam across my exposed skin for a few moments, taking it in. She can see where it's already peppered in a couple of large dark bruises. We have protective gear, which usually helps with this sort of thing, but the way I was hit, and then when the guy landed on me, he was able to get me pretty good.

"Oh my God! You shouldn't be out here right now. You need to be inside with ice and heat on that. Or at the clinic, so my mom can give you something for the pain. How can you even walk right now? I'd be doubled over in pain."

I shrug and continue to screw the lids on her jars. "I've been playing through pain since I was a kid. It's just something you do, especially when you want to win games. I've gotten so used to it over the years that this is nothing compared to some of the injuries I've had in the past. I'm fine, really. I just want to help you and not worry about my next game until I go to practice tomorrow afternoon."

She nods, busying herself by going behind me to wipe the jars down with a clean cloth before setting them in neat little stacks. We get them all boxed up with bows or put in various baskets where she wants. Before I know it, we're done with at least one item on her list she had been stressing over.

"I need to head up to the cabin. I want to chop down a tree to donate to the church, and then I'm going to grab some supplies we keep up there. We usually make the candy at the cabin since it's out of the way, but I don't want to be far from Dad with his injuries. I'm going to use the kitchen at home and store everything in the dining room until it's packaged and put into boxes, then it can come out to the barn until festival time. Next week, I'll work on the candles, and should be done with everything just in time for setup."

"Sounds like a good idea, let's go." I grab the closest chainsaw and follow her back outside to her father's truck. I place the chainsaw in the bed of David's truck and then hurry to open her driver's side door for her.

"Thank you," Winter shoots me a surprised glance, wearing a sweet smile, and my stomach flips. I'm relieved she's no longer attempting to completely ignore me like she was trying to before. She actually seems happy to have me here, and I keep getting butterflies in my gut nearly every time she glances in my direction.

The truck rumbles to life as I get in the passenger side. I slide onto the bench seat and quickly close my door to keep the cold out. I'm glad I still have some coffee left because this old pickup is like an ice box in the cab. I should've worn some warmer clothes, but in my defense, I thought we'd be in the barn or her parents' house all day when we weren't checking on the animals. Taking in the woman beside me, it looks like she wasn't planning on traipsing through the woods to get a tree today either.

"So you're donating a tree? Does your family do that every year?"

She remains focused on the snowy ground before us as she slowly drives the old pickup to the far side of their family farm. "No, my family has offered to, but different businesses usually beat us to it. Dad told me this morning that Mrs. Anderson, the woman who organizes the food pantry over there, had called and told him the tree donation had fallen through. She wanted to give us the chance to bring a tree down first because it's been a few years since our last."

I nod, thinking about small ways to help, and if I should contact my beverage sponsor to see if they'd be willing to do a donation. Being close to the holidays, a lot of companies are looking for affordable ways to be involved, and this could be the answer for them while also assisting small food pantries during some rough months. Since I'm in professional sports, I'm used to doing several different community charitable events per year. They're either organized by the team or others that have personally reached out, and I've taken an interest in. Anytime I hear about other people who don't have a hefty disposable income going out of their way to make contributions, I want to know more. If I'm able to step in and do anything for the cause their supporting, then I usually will. Even if it's simply sharing the charity on my socials, sometimes that's all it takes to get the right people involved and make a difference.

The drive to the cabin is quick; it's probably two miles or so away from the farm, and partially up the side of the closest mountain. Nothing too high up, just enough so when you're at the cabin, it's tucked away in the trees to make you feel like you're surrounded by nothing but the beautiful snowy wilderness. Everything out this way lies untouched in a serene way. The powdery white snow is thick and bright, with the tree branches hanging low, heavy from the added weight. As I take in the cozy little cabin, I understand why her family built it.

Am I crazy for imagining her here, with me, spending time alone together? I can picture a family running around, kids playing outside in the snow, and us finding a Christmas tree together, all way too easily. Fantasizing about sharing a future with her should throw up red flags for me, demanding I pump the brakes, but it's as easy as breathing. The realization I had in the locker room after my game hits me all over again, but this time it's stronger.

I want this.

And I only want it with *her*.

"I know it's going to be freezing inside there." Winter tilts her head toward the cabin once she's parked and we're standing outside the truck. "We should probably cut the tree down before grabbing the supplies, since it's beginning to snow again. I don't want the boxes to get wet while sitting in the bed, waiting for us to finish with the tree."

I tuck a strand of her hair behind her ear, as the urge to touch her whenever possible grows stronger. The move makes her pause, her lashes lowering as she stares up to meet my gaze, and I nearly lose myself in her. She's always beautiful, but out here, I swear she takes my breath away.

"I agree," I finally say, taking a step away to put a little distance between us so I can think again. "It always surprised me that your dad didn't open a tree farm out here with all this land your family owns. There are so many pines out here, he wouldn't have to plant many."

I grab the chainsaw and follow her down a path between the trees. She seems to know exactly where she's going, so this must be the place they always come to get their Christmas trees. I'm kind of surprised she's not playing carols on her cell as we walk; she's the type of woman that if we all had theme songs, hers would be *Walking in a Winter Wonderland*. That song is exactly why I started calling her *Winter Wonderland* when we were younger, and she'd shown up wearing all white to go ice skating with me. I thought she was the prettiest girl I'd ever seen that day, with her flushed cheeks and pink nose. After all this time, I can confirm she still holds that title in my heart.

"He's friends with the owner of the tree farm in Noelville, so he never wanted to take any business from them."

"Makes sense," I reply, and then we grow quiet as she strolls along. Our footsteps leave a path behind us in the perfect blanket of snow. I match my pace to hers, so I can walk next to her and take in the peacefulness of the woods. I can't remember the last time I went and cut down my own Christmas tree. It had to be the year before I started college.

Winter's arms flail suddenly, as a shriek escapes her. In the next moment, she pitches backward, her feet flying forward. I instantly drop the chainsaw and reach for her. Thankfully, because of hockey, my reflexes are quick enough that I'm able to grab her before she hits the ground.

Her eyes are wide, her chest heaving as I pull her up and make sure she's steady enough on her feet. I don't release her right away, as having her in my arms once again is what I've been thinking of nonstop since Thanksgiving. Her hands rest on my chest; her body pressed against mine, and it's the warmest I've felt all day. She does this to me somehow, in a way no one ever has before. She's a bit breathless as she manages to whisper, "Wow, good catch."

I gaze down at her, taking in her hot cocoa irises, while wishing she were already mine. That I could dip my head a bit, pressing my lips to hers. We're not there yet, so I'll take any closeness I can get from her in the meantime. "Are you okay?"

She nods, "Thank you." Her eyes land on my lips, making me wonder if she's imagining kissing me, too. If she would push me away, or pull me in for a deeper taste. "I see why you're so good on the ice. You're *fast*," she admits, her voice trailing off.

Needing to break up the moment before I do something that could possibly rush her before she's ready, I press a soft kiss to her forehead. Taking a step back, I promise, "I'm here anytime you need me." I wink, attempting to lighten the moment and release my hold on her. I turn for the chainsaw, grab it, and then hold out my elbow for Winter.

Much to my surprise, she takes it without a rebuke. She wraps her hand around me, holding on, as she walks a bit more carefully than she was before. She murmurs something else, but all I can think of is how I want to have her in my arms again, and that the time can't come soon enough.

How I want to kiss her and make her agree to finally be *mine*.

Sapphire Knight

CHAPTER TWELVE

WINTER

I was floating the entire time we were together to cut the tree down. I swear I don't think my feet touched the snow after he'd pressed his lips to my forehead and made my heart stutter. It was pure sweetness, and the way he'd stared at me, as if I was the brightest Christmas star he'd ever wished on...Well, it was enough to make me nearly lean in and kiss his lips. I held back, of course, but not because I didn't want to kiss him. The opposite, actually, and the reality has me a little worried if I'm being honest with myself. Sean is a professional hockey player, a very successful one who travels a lot for his job, and then there's also the fact that we don't live in the same city anymore.

However, I have these feelings I can't seem to shake that've been rushing back for him in abundance. No matter how much I silently fight them, they seem to keep building between us. I would be dumb to ignore it all, right?

We get the large pine tree loaded into the back of Dad's pick-up truck, and by we, I mean Sean, lifts it like it's his other day job. The man is made of pure muscle, I swear. I could watch him lift and flex all day long without complaint. "I'm glad we waited for the other supplies," I mention, lifting my gloved hand to catch some of the bright flakes that have covered the truck in a thick blanket of white already.

The snow started falling pretty quickly the moment we set out, trekking through the trees, to find the perfect pine to donate to the church. The flurries didn't bother me, though. I used to take the beauty of this place for granted as a kid, but I refuse to as an adult. Halfway through our walk, I stopped along our path and stared. Watching as the fluffy puffs drifted down, landing around us and over the trees. Sean had paused too, watching me for a moment before he realized I was simply taking in the moment. Then, he did the same.

I've read so many romance novels where the couples in the books watch the sunset together, but where are the stories that share the absolute peace and connectiveness that watching the snow fall can bring, when you're with the right person?

I flash a smile as I flick some snow from the side of the truck at the gorgeous man. He laughs, his brows raising in challenge, and I know if I hit him with some more snow, I'll be in for it. You don't grow up around here and not learn how to make a mean snowball. I have a feeling this talented hockey player isn't to be trifled with.

I raise my hands in surrender, "No more snow. Although you could probably use a little on that bruise you got from playing your last game."

He shakes his head, following me as I close the tailgate, and then he quickly bends. Before I have the chance to hop out of the way, he's stuffing a handful of snow at my neck and down my jacket. The icy chunk quickly melts its way lower over the sensitive skin on my back.

"Ah!" I scream from the jolt of coldness, following it up with a burst of giggles. "You are in for it! Just wait, when you're least expecting it, I'm going to get you back." I spin around with the promise, my smile beaming so widely it makes my cheeks hurt.

He chuckles, lunging forward to pull my beanie down over my face so I can't see. He teases, "I'm scared, Winter Wonderland. You have me shaking in my boots over here."

"You are such a brat!" I laugh, fixing my knitted hat back into place. It's white with fake pearls all over it in random spots and a fluffy puff at the top. I push on his bicep, being playful, but he doesn't budge an inch. *Geesh.*

My hands stay planted on his arm, feeling him flex the muscle underneath my hold, and suddenly I'm fully aware of how close we are, and that I'm still touching him. With a shaky exhale, I drop my hold and take a step back, shaking my head. I need to put some space between us before I lose my heart completely, and then he disappears to live out his hockey life after the holidays. I'll be forced back into my reality and feeling bitter all over again that I didn't get my chance with him.

"Let's grab the other stuff. It shouldn't be much, just a few boxes." I lead the way to the entrance of my family's cabin, with Sean quickly catching up. We take the two steps onto the tiny porch, and I immediately reach for the knob. The door sticks for a beat, probably from the freezing temps we've been hitting at night, so I lean against the wood, putting my weight into it until it finally gives.

"Brrr…I knew it was going to feel like a fridge in here." I comment, glancing around. I don't miss the sprigs of fake mistletoe hung up around the cabin in my perusal, but I choose to ignore them. Mom has been adamant about leaving them up all year long; she claims it's her way of sneaking extra kisses with Dad.

"How does it seem warmer outside right now?" Sean mutters, taking everything in. The shelves and mantle in the main room are overflowing with pictures of me and my siblings when we were younger. In each framed moment, we're busy fishing, making smores, telling spooky stories over a campfire, swimming, rowing a tiny boat out onto the lake, and a myriad of other activities. "You guys look happy."

I nod. "We had a good childhood, I was lucky." I leave it at that, knowing he lost his father at a kind of young age, and he struggled through the same years when I was living my best life. I don't want to see him hurt, and I wish there were a way he could've experienced what I did growing up. Our family has always been close, to the point that we did everything together. Not because we had to, but because we always wanted to. It's not most people's reality, and I know how lucky I am; that's why I'll always come home the minute my family calls.

"You were a cute kid," he says, picking up the framed photo with my face covered in chocolate, smiling widely.

"I helped Gram make a chocolate pie in that one," I comment, remembering how she'd made it an extra special treat by sneaking me mini marshmallows to dip in the pie filling. We were on spring break and had planted a ton of wildflowers that year. It's one of those cherished times I'll never forget and hope to recreate for my own grandchildren someday.

"Why do I get the feeling you were eating the chocolate and she was the one baking?" He teases, and I roll my eyes.

"Probably because that's exactly what I was doing," I admit. "Come on," I gesture to the hallway and point to the low ceiling that leads up to the boxes of supplies I still need. I could reach the small loop to the attic door for the ladder with a step stool, but why go to all the trouble when I have this giant man who can easily grab it for me?

Sean makes his way to where I am, only to stand directly in front of me in my personal space. I catch a whiff of his cologne being this close, and it takes every ounce of self-control I possess not to stare up at his impressive stature. He easily hooks the loop with his fingers and then carefully lowers the small door. Next, he grabs the ladder attached to the thick wood and lowers it until the feet securely rest on the floor.

"Thanks." My shoe lands on the first step, needing to get into the attic right this moment, before I end up trying to climb Sean instead. I quickly make my way up, poking my head in through the opening. "I know we stuck those boxes up here somewhere."

It's too dark to see what I need, but I know there's a flashlight Dad keeps in a cupholder that's screwed in place, to the right of the door. He did it so we'd never lose it as kids. I reach for the holder, jiggling the flashlight until it eventually comes free from the holder. A weird screech and bark sort of sound comes from my left. Then there's a *hiss*.

"What was that, Winter? Do you hear scratching?" Sean calls from below, effectively distracting me.

"Huh? Scratching? Where?" I ask, then something comes flying at me out of the dark, hissing and screeching angrily.

I scream as my body jolts backward to miss whatever the heck is after me and lose my footing in the process. The flashlight flies out of my hand, landing somewhere with a loud thump. My arms flail as I reach for anything to help, panicking in the process. My scream of surprise morphs into a shout of newfound fear as my feet slip off the rungs. My balance seems to disappear completely, and then, I'm falling.

Right into a pair of strong arms.

"Oof!" Leaves me, and then I'm meeting Sean's wide stare.

He holds me tightly to his strong frame, checking, "You okay? What just happened?"

I think he's breathing heavier than I am right now, and I'm the one who just fell from the freaking ceiling!

Shaking my head, I inhale and exhale, attempting to calm my racing heart. I'm a frazzled mess at the moment, and silently thanking the Lord that this beefy man was nosy enough to stand at the bottom of the ladder and ended up catching me. The landing could've hurt pretty badly had he not been right here. "I was attacked by something feral, and then nearly broke my neck, which is exactly what happened." I supply with a bit of dramatic flair.

"No bites? Scratches? Where did it get you?" His worried gaze scans over me from top to bottom.

"No, nothing."

He stops looking, meeting my eyes again. A smirk settles on his luscious lips, and so help me, I want to lean forward and suck his bottom lip between mine. It'd wipe that look off his face in an instant, while finally letting me have a taste. "So, you weren't actually attacked then?"

"I almost was, *thankyouverymuch*. Plus, I lost my balance. I'd like to see you go up there to battle the bear and get the boxes then, if we're not counting feral animal attacks unless we're bitten." He's still holding me princess style, and would it be weird if we just stayed like this? I need protection from animals who are chasing me, and he's the only tall person around.

"Considering I was nearly knocked out by the flying flashlight, I think my chances are good with whatever's up there."

"Be brave then, but I'm not driving you to the clinic to explain this to the moms. You'll have to deal with the rabies and tell your coach it was solely your fault." Not only that, but he'd have to ride in the bed of the truck. No way am I taking chances with him going all *zombie* on me.

He laughs loudly. "I'll take my chances, but I think if I end up getting bit, it's only fair you nurse me back to health." He winks and then carefully sets me down.

As soon as my feet are firmly planted on the floor, I'm racing to the couch. I climb up onto it like I used to as a kid, when my siblings and I would pretend the floor was either lava or covered in alligators.

Sean grabs the flashlight that ended up down the hallway somehow, and then I watch as his foot hits the bottom rung. I know one thing's for sure; no crazy critters are about to get my feet if something comes back down with the cocky athlete. He can handle that one all on his own. He begins to climb up, thankfully not asking me to spot him, because clearly, I've proven I'm not the best when it comes to balance.

A moment later, he's disappearing into the attic. "Aww," I swear I hear him say, and it has my curiosity piqued. "Aren't you a cute little lady. I'm grabbing a few boxes and that's it, okay? You won't be bothered, just keep warm."

"Who are you talking to?"

He doesn't reply. After a few minutes, he begins descending the ladder, somehow balancing two boxes as he does. He hops off the fourth rung, keeping the boxes secure, then he sets them down and lifts the ladder, closing the attic. He hasn't said a word yet, and I won't lie, my mind is spinning with possibilities over what he found up there.

Chapter Thirteen

Winter

"Uh, what was all that?" I point to the ceiling and gesture a bit wildly. "I swear I heard you talking to someone, and I'm just wondering how you made it out unscathed?"

"There's a momma raccoon up there with her babies. You scared her, so she was protecting little Timmy, Tot, and Tabitha."

"You named her babies?" My mouth is hanging open; I can feel it. Who is this man?

He shrugs, "May as well. Once she saw I was headed to the other side of the attic, she didn't pay me much attention."

"Um...that raccoon was hostile and ready to take a bite out of me moments ago. Now you're telling me she didn't even bat an eye when you went to grab the boxes?"

He shrugs again like it's no big deal. "Probably brought her kids up there to stay warm with the random snowfall. They won't bother you." He's talking about them as if she's a little old lady and her babies are my long-lost cousins or something, just as ridiculous. Here I am fearing for my life, while the animal whisperer in front of me is ready to invite her over for Sunday brunch.

With a huff, I ask, "Have you seen the videos of pet raccoons? There a menace, getting into everything. They know how to open refrigerators. *Refrigerators!* And I'm pretty sure it takes a tiny mastermind to figure that out."

"You watch raccoon videos?"

I wave him off, not ready to admit anything about all the animal videos I watch when I'm bored. "That's beside the point. Were those the only two boxes marked Christmas candy supplies and holiday market on them?"

He nods, and relief fills me knowing I won't have to venture back up into the attic anytime soon. I'll have to let Dad know, though, so he can try to get the new tenants out once he's healed and back to working the farm, or else they may tear the place up.

"Okay, let's get back home. My feet need defrosting by the fire before my toes decide to fall off." I move for the boxes, but he beats me to them, easily carrying both.

I hurry to open the door for him and follow him out, closing the sturdy wood door behind us. I watch his bubble butt as he walks, checking him out. Noting that even after he's helped me nearly all day with random stuff, he still manages to look the same as he did when he'd surprised me in the barn. There's not even a hair out of place, while he smells like a snack, and looks like one, too. *Gah.*

I'm thinking of that taut stomach of his when I nearly crash into his back while stepping down the stairs. I manage to quickly dodge to the side. "What's the matter?" My gaze shoots around the cleared area, wondering if we're having another run-in with a different animal. Hopefully not an actual bear this time.

"Please tell me you have a spare that I somehow missed when I was loading the tree in the back?"

"A spare?" I glance at the truck, not seeing what he's obviously noticed. "For what?"

"The tire is flat."

I jog over to Dad's truck, staring at the tire in question. As soon as I'm close enough, I kick the snow away from it. He's right. It's not only a little flat,1.2.. either; the rim is basically sitting on the frozen, hard ground. There's no way I can drive it back like this, even just to the farm, without seriously messing something up. The road home is snowy, icy, full of potholes, and who knows what else, because it's not an actual road. It's the same path we always use to get to the cabin, so the ground has been worn down, but there's no gravel or pavement.

He opens the tailgate and sets the boxes of supplies down on it, shifting the tree from side to side, peering underneath it. I guess he's checking for a spare he thinks has magically been tucked away under the branches. Next, he ducks his head below, looking underneath the bed, but it's useless. I already know there's no tire anywhere. Dad is notorious for taking the spare tire out when he's moving something, and then forgetting to put it back in. "No tire."

"No tire," I echo, confirming. "Dad pulls it out all the time and forgets to put it back in." I tug my cell free from my jacket pocket only to discover I have zero bars. No surprise there with the snow-covered mountains surrounding us and the flurries making it hard to see more than ten feet in front of us. "I've got no cell signal either," I call out as I shiver through a gust of icy air.

I hurry to the closest tree, standing under it to help block the snow from landing on me. I wish I'd grabbed my heavier coat before we left, but in my defense, I was expecting this to be a quick trip here and back. I had no idea I was going to get caught up in the moment and end up spending extra time out here with Sean.

He tries his phone, but he actually has service. Weird how that works, and it may be time I switch providers. He calls someone, walking around the truck to check each tire. "Hey Doug. Winter's dad's truck has a flat, and we're not at the farm. Are you free to swing by and grab it since David is still on crutches back at the house? You can add it to my bill."

He glances at me for a beat as he comes to stand under the tree, his brow furrowing as he listens to whatever Doug is saying. "You're joking, it's been a few hours, tops, since we got out here. Town was fine this morning when I left my mom's place. No way. *Jesus.* Okay, yeah, thanks. We'll figure something out. Stay safe out there."

My body starts to shiver more, making me realize it's from a drop in the temperature, and not just from walking outside into a random gust of freezing wind. I take in our surroundings the best I can, noticing how the snow has been piling up quickly compared to when we first arrived. It seems to keep getting worse as time passes.

"No luck?" My teeth chatter, and I burrow deeper into my thin, knitted scarf Gram made for me years ago. I've worn it so many times, it's practically threadbare at this point.

He shakes his head, cheeks flushed. It reminds me of what he looked like when we were younger, and I'd watch him play in one of the junior league games. "According to Doug, the roads are closed in town until the plow can go through. I guess the village put out a snow warning yesterday for today, which wasn't going to be a big deal, but..."

"But?"

"The news said that the previous snow prediction was met with a new shifting storm today on top of it, coming in from the east. Now, we're getting a record number of precipitation for the amount of time that's passed."

"Oh, no." My eyes widen, shifting to stare at the truck again as the roof gets covered more and more. It probably wouldn't make it back to the house now, even if the tire wasn't flat. Having Sean around as a distraction hasn't helped with my outer awareness, let alone with me keeping track of how much time has passed.

"I don't think it's as bad over here yet, as Doug was saying. The mountains are probably helping some," he rationalizes. "The plows are about to go out to hopefully get it cleared enough so folks can at least make it home before the worst of it hits."

"This is crazy. How are we going to get back to the farm? I can't drive Dad's old truck in this." I gesture to the area we drove in from, "Look how deep it is over there!"

"I know." He agrees with a frown, and then he's calling someone else.

"David?"

It's Dad. He'll know what to do; he always does.

He listens for a minute, then replies, "Yeah, I just heard. The truck tire's completely flat, and the spare isn't in the back anywhere. We're both okay, still at the cabin. Should we walk? I'm worried because we're not dressed for blizzard weather." He glances my way, taking me in from top to bottom.

He continues after a moment, "No, she's in her lighter jacket. I am too. Should we just try it?" He nods at whatever Dad's saying while flicking his gaze between me and the cabin. "I can feel the temperature change, too; the wind gusts are no joke. Don't worry, we'll figure it out. Are you going to be okay? Do you have enough wood in the house for the living room in case you lose power?"

He grabs my hand, lacing our fingers together, and begins walking toward the cabin. He gently tugs for me to follow, which I quickly oblige.

"Okay, good. I'll get our wood stocked up right now; she'll be safe with me. You have my word. Yes, Sir, you too. Talk soon." He hangs up with a sigh, and he's no longer the carefree hockey player I've come to expect. In its place is a super-serious Sean, ready to do whatever my dad told him to.

"What did Dad say?" I question as he slows his pace enough to wrap his arm around me. He tucks me in close to his chest, his bulk helping to block the wind and keep me warm as we walk together.

"Our moms are stuck at the clinic. Your grandparents' place got hit first, so I'm guessing they have more snow than us right now, and the temperature has just dropped fifteen degrees in the last forty minutes, according to the weather channel your dad has been watching. He's worried that if we try to walk back in this, it'll get worse before we have a chance to make it to your parents' house."

"I hope everyone is okay. Dad will worry himself sick over Mom not being there with him."

As soon as we're on the porch, he leans against the front door and uses his bulk so it opens right away this time. The last thing I want to do at the moment is release him, but I do, slipping out from under his arm. He quickly shoves the door closed behind us, and I exhale a sigh of relief from being out of the bone-chilling wind once again. It was so beautiful earlier, but now, it's just plain nasty outside.

He heads for the fireplace, mentioning, "Our moms are waiting for the snow plows to go by so they can follow it to the farm's driveway. Their plan is to get that far and then walk the driveway, since the plow won't go up it. Luckily, they don't have any patients tonight. David wants us to stay put, he said to check the wood stack, but that there's plenty of food and blankets here. He said your mom is going to drive the tractor to get your grandparents since it's close, and then your grandfather will drive the tractor here with some warmer clothes and to grab us, if possible. We just have to sit tight for a night."

I nod, worry filling me that Mom, Gram, and Pop aren't all at the house together. It's always the plan when there's a big storm heading to town. They've lived here forever, so they are more than capable of taking care of themselves, but they're my family, so it's natural to be worried. Especially when Dad is too injured to help, and he's the one everyone depends on the most around here since Dasher joined the military and had to move away. I wish my brother were here to help out right now instead of being busy playing soldier.

Thankfully, the farm has generators and supplies for this sort of thing, so hopefully everyone makes it there soon, and Dad isn't left alone. I can't believe Mom and Calla are going to try and walk the driveway; it's at least a mile to the house from the road, and that's only if it gets plowed that far. However, knowing Mom, her SUV is loaded down with various supplies, including blankets. I'd bet she even has a spare tire like she's supposed to.

My gaze lands on Sean again, taking in his tussled hair. He ran his hand through it a moment ago, making me wish I could do the same. I haven't been able to peel my attention off him ever since he showed up this morning, and now we're going to be here overnight.

Alone in the cabin.

Together.

CHAPTER FOURTEEN

SEAN

I take in Winter's worried expression, wishing we were already back at the farm, so I could handle everything needing to be done for her father, as well as get our families to the house safely. I may not be able to do what I want right now, but the least I can do is show Winter she's safe with me.

"I promised your father I'd keep you safe, and I meant it. I'll do everything I can to make sure you're warm tonight, and I get you back home with all ten toes still intact."

Her teeth sink into her lower lip as she nods, moving next to me at the fireplace. I immediately begin setting the wood up properly, tucking kindling in where I need it to get a good burn going. I make sure the vent inside the top of the fireplace is open and then strike one of the long matches kept off to the side in a tin.

"You can take the boy out of the mountains, but not the mountains out of the boy, hm?" She comments and gestures to the fire that's quickly catching over the wood. It helps that the wood's been sitting for a while; it's nice and dry.

With a smirk, I move the protective screen in front of the fireplace. "I was camping with my father before I could walk. The same with ice skating. There's no way I'm forgetting how to build a decent fire in the cold. Speaking of the cold, you stay inside and defrost. I need to check out the wood stack your father mentioned."

"I'll get the woodstove going and hunt down some coffee or something to help us warm up, too. I should probably see what we have to eat around here, as well."

"Sounds good." Although I know her well enough that she won't be thrilled with just coffee. She likes the really sweet frou-frou stuff, and always has, so hopefully they have plenty of sugar stored around here as well.

I head back out into the cold and off to the left side of the cabin. There's a small enclosed area built onto the side, and like any experienced farmer who's lived in the mountains for far too long, it's set up for hunting, storing meat, and stacked with plenty of wood already split for the fireplace. There's even a dry cellar dug out in the ground to keep veggies fresh. I'll have to come back out on the next days I have off, when the snowstorm has passed, and I'm able to chop up some more wood to refill what we end up using. I have a feeling it'll be a lot, since it's supposed to get colder than usual tonight with several feet of snow still heading our way.

Using a tarp I find folded, I lay it open outside the storage room, and load it with wood. Once it's full, I pull the pile using the tarp to help it slide across the snow and up to the porch. It's not an easy feat, but I manage because it'll make it quicker for me when I'm going in and out of the cabin, as I bring the wood inside to last us throughout the night.

When I step inside, I'm greeted with the scent of chocolate permeating the air, along with the fresh fire that's now blazing in the living room. "Something smells good," I comment while bringing in my first load of chopped wood. It's starting to warm up in the small space, too, which is exactly what we need.

"I found some hot chocolate mix. I just added it to the boiling water on the stove, so you must be smelling that." She responds while watching as I neatly stack the new logs beside the fireplace.

"Hot chocolate sounds even more delicious than coffee at the moment." I grin, thinking the only thing that would make it any better would be tasting it on her tongue. Rather than admit as much, I continue with my job.

I move back and forth as quickly as possible to keep as much heat in the cabin as I can. After all of the woods inside, I fold the tarp back up. Put it in the same spot I found it, then close up the small storage room, and head back inside.

The first thing I notice is that Winter has removed her gloves, hat, and jacket, and is standing in front of the wood stove. She must be feeling warmer already, which brings me a ridiculous amount of joy for some reason. Her cheeks are still pink, but it suits her, somehow making her more beautiful than she already is.

"We need to cover the windows in here with some extra blankets to keep the heat in," I mention, already heading for the hall to search out any supplies we can use. This place is set up for mild weather, especially when it comes to winter, so I doubt our heat will stay inside for very long unless we help winterize it a bit.

I close each room's door as I exit it, my hands overfilled with quilts her Gram must've made throughout the years. I set them on the couch, and then join her in the kitchen again. "The rooms won't stay warm, so I'm thinking I should bring a mattress in and put it in front of the couch. That way, we can sleep with the fire close by. I'll take the couch."

She scoffs, immediately shaking her head in protest. "There's no way you can sleep on the couch, it's way too small. We can share the mattress and the blankets. Besides, we'll stay warmer if we're together, right? Body heat and all that…"

I'm silent as I nod, a bit stunned that she's willing to share the bed with me in her family's cabin. Maybe it's the sign I've needed all along, to know she'll be okay with me taking the next step between us and finally kissing her. God, just the thought of her mouth on mine gives me crazy zings all over. However, I don't know if I should kiss her right now, and possibly end up making her feel awkward if I'm reading her signals wrong. Maybe I'll wait until we're not snowed in a small cabin together, without the option to leave suddenly…You know, just in case it doesn't go the way I want it to. At least with a kiss planned to happen soon, I'll finally know if we're headed in the direction I'm hoping for.

"I just remembered the boxes we left on the tailgate. I'm going to go grab them so your supplies don't get ruined."

Her face lights up, telling me she'd forgotten about them as well. "Oh yeah, good thinking. Did my dad tell you there's a generator behind the cabin? It's not powerful enough to run everything in here, but it'll give us some lights since it's getting darker outside, and we can plug in one of the space heaters to help with the storm tonight."

"He didn't, but I'll check it out."

"Thank you, Sean. What you're doing, it means a lot."

"I'll always take care of you, and besides, we've got this. No worries." I promise and walk outside.

I'm finally getting a second chance with the one woman I've always wondered about; she has no idea I'll do just about anything for her. Hopefully, after this Christmas, she'll realize I'm not the same young guy stepping to the side so easily. She's making me work for her time, and I'm enjoying every minute of proving to her that I can handle whatever she throws at me. I guess that's the difference between being a man and a boy, a man knows what he wants and is willing to do what it takes to reach the sweet reward in the end.

I'm on my way back to the door, boxes in hand, when my phone rings. I quickly set the festival supplies down inside the front door and pull my phone from my pocket, noticing I finally have a couple of service bars again. *It's my agent.* We check in monthly unless he has some new sponsorship deals for me to consider. If so, then we end up talking more, so a company must've reached out to him.

"Hey Spencer, how's it going?" I greet as soon as I swipe across my screen to accept the call.

"Spruce, I'm glad to catch you." He responds, calling me by my last name like everyone in my professional life does.

"I'm in the valley right now, so my service can drop at any time," I warn. "Did we get a new sponsorship offer? If so, I'll have to wait at least a day; a storm is hitting right now, and I'm about to be snowed in at a cabin. Would you let Coach know what's going on? I may need you to find me a helicopter willing to pick me up from the farm I'm staying at, so I can make it in time for the game. I'm pretty sure I'm going to miss my flight tomorrow, so we'll have to go another route." Not to mention the practices I'm missing, but there's nothing I can do at the moment.

"Spruce," he interrupts. "Hold on, man, don't worry about a chopper right now. If I need to find a pilot to fly you out of there, I will, but some things have changed with your contract."

I instantly stop my pacing that I didn't realize I was doing in the first place, and stare out of the cabin's window. I need to hurry up and cover it with a quilt to help keep the cold air out. I swear the snow looks deeper than when we came inside, but I know it can't be possible. "What do you mean by changes to my contract?"

I hear Winter draw in a swift breath at my words, so I step outside. This way, she doesn't hear me, in case I'm not going to like what Spencer has to say. I make my way toward the back of the cabin, easily finding the generator. I need to check the gas and see if there's a prime button I have to press before attempting to start it.

"Look, I tried to negotiate, but the Pines, they..." He answers, trailing off.

I'm distracted as I lift the wood covering to find that the generator has a full tank of gas. Which isn't very surprising, considering David seems to have everything well stocked out here. I grab the pull cord, giving it a good tug, and it fires right up. The loud rumble makes me hurry to place the wood cover back over it again, and then jog back around to the front of the cabin.

Huffing out a breath from the cold, I ask, "What? I thought my contract was solid for the next few years, then we were going to revisit the retirement option."

"Your contract *was* solid, but there are always clauses in it."

"*Was* solid?" My voice rises a touch as I repeat the words, and my heart starts to beat a bit frantically. *What does he mean, it was?* "We may've lost the game the other night, but it's not because of my performance. I scored! I may be getting older in the league's standards, but I'm still matching or beating everyone else in my position. You know I make sure to stay up with those stats."

"I know, and it has nothing to do with your performance. The opposite, actually. I'm always fielding calls for other teams who are interested in shaking up your contract so you'll come play for them, but we've kept you with the Pines because their GM and owner are so good about working with your schedule when going home and stuff, they cater to your special training and requests."

I cut him off, "That I've earned. I've played my tail off for the Pine's since college, and hold one of the highest scoring records for the team. Those special requests were because I've earned the time, and they agreed, it's in my contract." I state, my muscles locked up at whatever these changes could possibly mean.

"You don't have to tell me that, buddy, I already know. Your stats have helped us negotiate each time your contract opens up; you've made my job easy in that department. But like I said, and please Sean, let me finish."

I remain quiet, my fingers pinching the bridge of my nose as I close my eyes and tip my head down. I was finally in a position to hopefully start a life with Winter, and now something is changing. It could be big; I can feel it, and the buildup has me growing anxious. Did the Pines decide to release me early, and now I'm going to be pushed into retirement whether I'm ready to go or not? I need time to come up with a plan if so, they can't just blindside me after the years I've dedicated to this team. Besides, why would they willingly push off the ice when my last contract was so lucrative? They'd lose out on the multi-millions they've already agreed to pay me over the course of my contract.

CHAPTER FIFTEEN

SEAN

"Like I said, this has nothing to do with your performance; it's the opposite, actually. You're a household name with proven stats, you're well-liked amongst your teammates, have huge brand sponsorships, multiple individual awards, the works…" Someone asks him something in the background, and he quietly responds. It's probably his assistant, he has a few, as he's busy twenty-four-seven most days, it seems. "The change is coming from the team itself. The Pines are in serious financial trouble. I don't have the exact details at the moment, but they're having to put up their biggest, most expensive players for trade, in hopes they can recoup funds in contract buy-outs and not go bankrupt."

"Wow." My eyes spring open in surprise at the news, and I glance out at the trees surrounding the place. Being secluded like this makes it feel like I'm not on the farm at all anymore, but somewhere peaceful and untouched. The team going bankrupt and needing to sell off contracts is literally the last thing I was expecting him to say. Maybe being out here for a night is what I need to help cut out some of the noise that this scandal will surely bring. If I were in New York right now, I wouldn't be able to leave my apartment because the media and paparazzi would be camped out front, waiting to bombard me. They'd try to force a comment out of me, no matter how ruthlessly they had to pursue it, and that's something I don't want to have to deal with.

"I know. The announcement is all over the media at the moment, but I'm guessing if you're snowed in at a cabin somewhere, then you wouldn't be watching what I am right now."

"No, I haven't seen anything. So, they're trading me." I say the words out loud, the news sitting like a lead weight in my gut.

I've been under contract with the Pines pretty much since I was just a reckless kid, taking more hits than was good for me. They'd signed me off the junior league that I was playing for at the time, from a few towns over. I'd started in that league when I was fifteen, and played for a couple of years while making some career-long connections and learning a lot, then came the Pines contract.

At the time, I had already been planning on playing college ice hockey as soon as I graduated, and had three years of Juniors under my belt. Several universities had reached out at that point, offering me full-ride scholarships from a young age, when the Pines call came through.

They wanted me badly enough to agree to sign me on a conditional contract.

The owner of the Pines had two main conditions: the first being that after two years of my playing for the college team, I would officially leave it behind for the NHL. He believed I could gain some valuable skills in my playing time, while also having a little more time to mature before being hit with the responsibilities of the pros. The second condition was that my contract was only valid if I didn't sustain any career-altering injuries that would ultimately affect how I performed for the team. It was a gamble, but I was young and went all in. I attended my two years in person at the university before moving to New York, as agreed. After that, in order for me to get my actual degree, I had to finish my classes online. It was tough, but I followed it through, knowing it was my mother's wish for me to have more education under my belt.

My entire professional career has been with one team only, and it hasn't escaped me how lucky I've been to have a franchise believe in my athletic ability so strongly from a young age to keep me with their team for so long. With a sigh, I ask, "What's the next move? Where do we go from here?"

"I'm going to keep working things on my end. My phone has been ringing off the hook all day with teams wanting to take over your contract, so you'll fall on your feet. I have no doubts."

Relief instantly hits me, and it's in this moment, I know I'm not ready to retire. At least not until I work through my full contract length. I've been fortunate to stay as healthy as I have, so that I can still think ahead to playing professional hockey in general.

On the other side of the coin, my being traded could put an end to any chance I may possibly have with Winter. I could be traded to Canada or Florida, or anywhere else across the country, and not be able to fly home so often. Depending on how well that team does, I could go months without really seeing her. The Cup is the ultimate goal in hockey, always, but will she still be waiting for me when the season is finally over? Winter isn't like me; she isn't meant to be away from her family for long periods of time, and she'd be miserable if she were.

"Which teams?"

"I have nine interests for you to review, and it hasn't been a full day yet. The Pines agreed they are willing to work with the players being traded, so you all can go to whatever team you want. Of course, that condition is only valid if the other teams expressing interest have high enough offers on the board for you all. The GM is a complete wreck over this. He finally has his dream team, and now he's having to watch you all be traded off."

"I can imagine, Jim's a good guy. Okay, how much time do I have before everything happens?"

"Forty-eight hours from the teams submitted offers, but I'll get a hold of everyone who has contacted me so far. I'll let them know you're in the middle of a snowstorm, to see if they will extend their offer times."

My shoulders relax a touch at hearing he already has a plan, but I should expect nothing less. He's paid well to keep my career together, and so far, he's done a great job at it. "Good. I want to review the terms and teams closest to home first. If I can no longer train at the Blizzards' arena during the season, I want to at least be able to squeeze in a few flights home whenever possible."

"I got it. I'll contact everyone and let them know what's going on in case they try to reach out to you directly. I'll have my assistant put the list together, and we'll add to it if anyone else submits an offer. Are you open to negotiating a new contract at all?"

I release a heavy sigh. I thought I wasn't going to have to worry about this again for a couple of years. Contract negotiations can be very stressful, especially when you want to go somewhere specific and are aware of your worth as a player in the league. "I'd prefer to keep the terms we already negotiated for."

"I understand that, but if they want to offer an extension and more money, are you willing to hear the teams out?"

"Yes, of course. Email me the info and I'll read through it as soon as I can."

"This is important, Spruce. As soon as the snow lets up enough, get home to check your inbox so you don't end up on a team you're not happy with. The Pines need cheaper players to fill slots and cash to pay bills, so they'll be making moves as soon as possible. I don't think they'll be as patient as the interested teams will be."

"I understand. Thanks for taking care of it."

"You bet, buddy. Stay safe, and let me know if I need to send in a helicopter to pick you up. In the meantime, try to take advantage of the snowstorm and get some rest in since you're not playing your next game. Ice your knees and ankles. Oh, and those ribs where you took that hard hit. I'm sure the new team you end up on will want you there immediately, and will be expecting you to be game day ready."

"Alright. I'll talk to you soon," I answer and hang up once he says his goodbye.

I tuck my phone away and leave from my spot under the tree where I seem to get the best signal strength. I should go back inside, but instead I sit on the small porch, staring off into nothing. The cold sinks through my pants underneath me, but I'm thinking too hard at the moment to truly feel it. All in a day, I went from worrying about a storm and kissing Winter, to stressing over my career and wondering if I'll even be around here enough to have the future I was starting to dream of.

I rake my hands through my hair, tugging on the ends as I try to come up with some sort of an answer. The unknown is nerve-wracking when you thought you finally had things figured out and a plan in motion. Life can change at the drop of a hat, and knowing I may miss my chance with Winter all over again because of this has me feeling a bit defeated inside. I should tell her what's happening, be upfront with everything, and the changes that I could be facing. However, if I say something, and she puts her walls up all over again, I'll be heartbroken. Asking her to come with me wherever I may end up is out of the question right now. I won't put that sort of pressure on her when she already has enough to deal with at the farm.

My back-and-forth thoughts are interrupted by the cabin's front door being opened behind me. The creak from the rusty hinges being frozen while Winter gives it a decent tug is hard to miss. I should see if there's some WD-40 or grease around here to fix that before I leave. "Hey," her soft voice calls. "You okay out here? It's freezing." I'm quiet for a moment before she says, "Sean, you're shaking. Please come in and warm up."

I nod and stand, then brush the snow off my clothes. Turning to her, I meet her concerned stare. "Yeah, you're right. I was just getting too cold."

"You were outside for a while, and I started to get a little worried. You're not in trouble for missing practice or something, right?" She asks as I follow her back into the cabin, closing the door behind us.

The warmth hits me, and I'm glad to find it's no longer cold, so she can relax. She has her boots off now, her thick wool socks on display. They remind me of a knitted Christmas sweater, and I don't know why I find them so cute. Maybe because they're on Winter's feet, and I seem to think everything about her is either adorable or beautiful.

I take the dark green, speckled mug she offers, the heat from it instantly warming my hands. The steamy scent drifts up to my nose, and I remember she said she'd found some hot chocolate earlier to make us. "This smells delicious."

"It's *so* good," she agrees with a small smile and refills her mug. She adds a candy cane to her cup and then hands me one for mine.

I can't remember the last time I had an actual candy cane. I suck on the red and white stick for a beat, the intensely sweet peppermint flavor exploding over my tongue. It's the best way to drink hot cocoa, and one thing Winter and I have always agreed on. I follow her to the couch and sit beside her.

She plops down in the corner, shifting her body so she's facing me, and I automatically pull her feet onto my lap. Her brows go up at my move, but she doesn't mention anything about it. "So your agent called?" She asks, no doubt noticing how quiet I'm being.

I'm not a huge talker anyhow, but when I'm thinking hard over something, I've been known to be the silent type. I nod, not wanting to come off as rude, but I'm also not ready to tell her what Spencer said and possibly ruin the moment. I go for a subject change. "I hope you weren't too upset with me having your car delivered. You haven't brought it up, which I figured you would've."

"Thanks for reminding me. Imagine my surprise when a tow truck came down the driveway, and Doug, who we went to school with, had my car attached to the back."

"A good surprise?"

"I mean, I didn't have to venture out in a tractor with no heat, having absolutely no idea how to get my car back. Aside from the bright idea of attaching a chain to some random part of the vehicle and then praying that when I pulled the car, it didn't completely fall apart. So, yeah, it was good."

I'm mentally patting myself on the back while sipping my hot chocolate. With my free hand, I lightly massage her feet, pulling her little toes until the knuckle pops, and it makes her giggle. She's ticklish on her feet, that much I remember from before. "I was wondering if Doug would fess up about who hired him." And, it looks like I was right about him not being able to keep it a secret.

"Yeah. The secret Santa was a bold move on your part," she comments dryly.

I quietly chuckle at the look she sends me. The one with her brows raised and her lips pursed into a smirk. I'm about to apologize, trying to think of the best thing to say when she shoots me a mock glare, making me keep my mouth shut for the moment.

"I especially liked how you pocketed my keys without asking, and distracted me with a cappuccino. Speaking of, were you up to something earlier when you brought drinks? Maybe I should be keeping my eye on you."

I groan, dropping my head back to glance at the ceiling. It makes her laugh, which I kinda adore. It's the sweetest sound, and I'd love nothing more than to hear it all the time. "Uh-oh, should I have kept quiet?"

She shakes her head as she shifts her foot to push against my leg. I begin to rub her foot again, taking the hint. I got distracted and quit moving my hand, but obviously, she's paying closer attention than I am since she noticed right away. "No, I'm glad you did. Dad was impressed, I'll say that much."

"Yeah, but…*were you?*"

The playful sparkle in her gaze tells me she wants to give me some more grief over it, and so help me, my lips tip into a smirk. She's spicy, and boy, do I enjoy every minute of it.

SAPPHIRE KNIGHT

Chapter Sixteen

Winter

I watch as Sean carries the mattress into the living room, thinking of our earlier conversation. He never did share what the call with his agent was about, but something more important happened, anyhow. He showed me his cards by admitting that my opinion on him fixing my car is the one he cares about. Not anyone else's, just *mine*.

Sean Spruce *likes* me.

He hasn't kissed me yet, and it was starting to make me wonder if I'm the only one feeling the connection growing between us. The bits of flirting we've shared, along with all of his helpfulness lately, have been giving me green flags. However, without him making an actual move on me or even talking about potential feelings, I can't help but get in my own head over what I want to be happening, versus what's actually happening. I've been getting the vibe from him that he wants me, and now, I'm fairly confident he's crushing on me just as strongly as I am with him.

When he was staring at my lips earlier, it made me want to lean in and kiss him so badly, but I held myself back. I can't help it that I've had my guard up, trying to protect myself this time around. I don't want another broken heart to deal with, especially at Christmastime, because that has to be the worst. Besides, I wouldn't have been able to look him in the eye again if I'd gone for it, and he ended up not wanting the same thing.

After our chat, with him wanting to know if I was impressed by my car being delivered, well, it opened my eyes a bit more. It's not only me picking up on the chemistry between us, and I've decided that I won't let another opportunity pass me up. If he gives me the same sexy smolder from earlier, or even starts to lean in, I'm planting my mouth on his. I'm going to finally put myself out of this pent-up, sweet misery that won't seem to stop growing inside of me.

I continue to stare, unable to focus my attention on anything but him at the moment. He carefully maneuvers the queen-sized mattress from the closest room until it's in front of the fireplace. He turns back to grab the sheets, blankets, and an armful of pillows. I did offer to help, but like the capable man Sean is, he politely turned me down and suggested I stay on the couch and keep warm.

Did I mention the guy is sweet? Total heartthrob, with a work ethic like no other. No wonder he's done so well for himself in hockey.

Not only is he a skilled player, but he's willing to put in the work it takes to be more than just an average athlete.

"You're doing good work over there," I comment, cheering him on while keeping my eyes pinned to all of his glorious muscles shifting and flexing beneath his waffle-knit thermal Henley. It's just tight enough to show the good stuff, while at the same time not coming off as a schmedium squishing him in. I won't lie, when he peeled off his jacket earlier and slipped his boots off by the door, I may've stared a little too hard then as well. One thing's for certain: he's not as lanky as he used to be, and it makes me want to send a thank-you card to whoever came up with his workout regimen. They're out here doing the Lord's work for us ladies, for sure.

"Yeah, yeah." He waves me off and shakes his head, almost as if he's well aware that I've been ogling him this entire time and he's not calling me on it.

Eventually, I hop up from the couch and head for the kitchen to see what I can scrounge up for us to eat. There are plenty of canned veggies and some soups, along with other foods that stay good for a longer period of time. Crackers, marshmallows, peanut butter, noodles, and other random items fill the pantry shelves. We don't come up here as much as we did when we were kids, since all of our schedules are out of whack, so the pantry and cabinets aren't stocked up like they used to be.

"We've got stuff for s'mores!" I call over my shoulder as I shift stuff around to see what else may be tucked away.

"I've never had s'mores."

"Um, you're kidding, right?"

"Nope. Not something my mom thought was a good idea. Boys and sticky sugar aren't always a clean option when you're a busy mom without much help."

Shoot, I didn't even think of that.

"We are *so* having s'mores tonight. It's going to change your life." And his coaches will end up hating me, as I slowly tank Sean's diet all in one day of being stuck in a cabin with me. I go for the most edible meal, which happens to be the cans of soup. It's not a five-star meal that I'm sure he's used to at this point in his life, but with some crackers, it'll keep us warm and from starving, so it's a winner in my book.

"I'm going to hold you to that," he replies as I busy myself opening the cans. I add the soup to a small pot and heat it over the woodstove. We've had this woodstove in here my entire life, so I learned to cook on it when I was a little girl. My parents were good about giving us so many different life experiences mixed with useful knowledge, and it never really hit me until right now.

Sean moves around the cabin, covering the windows with blankets and pushing a few throw pillows against the bottom of the front door. He's doing everything in his power to make sure I'm warm, comfortable, and well taken care of. It's got me looking at him with heart eyes, wondering why I was so adamant about staying away from him when we first ran into each other. I'm also finding myself wishing I'd made it a point to see him sooner, rather than nursing a fragile heart where he's concerned, for too long. We could've been friends for years, maybe even given dating another shot.

I ladle the soup into a bowl for each of us, grab two sleeves of crackers, and bring them to the kitchen table that's probably older than me. Once I set everything down, I grab a few spoons and a roll of paper towels to use for napkins. "Dinner's ready. Don't judge my reheating skills; I didn't have the stuff to make it from scratch. I'm a poor first date." I joke.

"Mm, it smells good, and after our busy day, I'm starving. Regardless of whether it's scratch-made or not, I'm grateful you heated it for us."

We sit next to each other, close enough that our arms graze against each other every time we move them. With each brush, as we carefully dive into our steaming dinner, I grow more and more aware of his presence beside me. I want to just dump the soup and climb onto his lap instead.

"I wanted to thank you. For the gift in my car. The keychain was thoughtful, and I love it. The angel was a sweet touch."

"I wanted to surprise you with something. When I had to leave town for my games, there was a gift shop at the airport of our first layover. We had enough time to basically get off and stretch our legs while the plane refueled, and I found the small shop near our gate. One of the main draws was the *create your own keychain*. They had it set up as a souvenir sort of thing, but I managed to pick out those charms." He shrugs, playing it off. "I was excited when it came together like it did."

"And the angel? The words on the back?" I can't help but ask.

"The woman was able to laser it for me. I know it's probably something silly, but it seemed like a good idea at the time."

"Are you kidding? Sean, it's beautiful and incredibly sweet. The gift was unexpected and thoughtful; it means a lot to me."

He tips his head down, his soup way more interesting as he quietly murmurs, "I'm glad, because *you being safe means a lot to me*. The W on it with the gemstones I sourced from a jeweler. I sent them a picture of the keychain and other charms, and they made sure it was the right size and tone, so it all matches."

"You're telling me the gemstones on my keychain are actually real stones and I'm supposed to keep it on a keychain?" That had to cost him a fortune! I thought it was just a sentimental gift, inexpensive, but meaningful. I would've loved it just as much if they were fake, but finding out he got it specially from a jeweler and somehow managed to get it to Doug to leave in the car all in the matter of a couple of days means he must've spent top dollar to make it happen.

"Yeah, they are. I wanted it to be special. I've enjoyed getting to spend time with you since you've been home. Then I practically barged in on your festival plans, you had to deal with me and my mom crashing your family Thanksgiving, and now we're snowed in here together. It's the least I could do, so you know how much this time has meant to me."

Jesus Christ, I just want to lean over and kiss the man like crazy. Shove his chair back, straddle his lap facing him, and lay a juicy one on him. Then we can work on peeling off these offensive clothes until he and I are left skin to skin. I would thoroughly enjoy the chance to properly say thank you to the hockey God right now, if given the chance.

"I won't lie…I was skeptical at first, but you've grown on me. I've enjoyed spending time with you, too. And, if I'm really being honest, my tinsel would've been in one helluva tangle if you hadn't shown up and decided to help me out at every turn this trip has tossed at me."

"No blizzard on your checklist this trip, I take it?"

"Or sliding on the ice, ditching my car, no cell service, no best friend, an injured dad, no siblings here to help shoulder their share, then the bank car robbers, flat tires, oh yeah, and me almost biffing it several times. You've turned into some kind of knight in shining armor. I'm apologizing in advance for whatever else you get drug into."

"It hasn't seemed bad to me; it's been the opposite."

Lord, sweet six-pound tiny baby Jesus in a little manger, this man is gunning to be the sweetest Christmas cookie this season at this rate. Like a big ol' dollop of maple syrup, I just want to lick him from top to bottom.

He hums with appreciation after he's devoured half the bowl of his soup, "Mmhm. I was right. You did a good job."

I preen a bit at his praise.

This is not an ideal first date, *if this were an actual date*, but it's simple, and I can appreciate that fact, too. It might help if I turn on some music or something to break up the silence when we're not talking. I could've added some candles to the table, too; maybe it would've made it a little more romantic. I wonder if he'll kiss me tonight? If not, I may have to sneak at least one in before we fall asleep.

"Hey, Sean? Can I ask you something? It has to do with our past, so if you don't want me to go there, I won't."

"You can ask me anything." He meets my gaze, watching as I slurp chicken and rice soup from my spoon. I don't know how he wolfed his down so fast, because mine's still a bit hot.

I set my utensil down, nerves twisting my belly with what I want to know. "When you broke up with me and moved away, was it because you had met someone else?"

His brows raise, and I can tell my question has caught him completely off guard. He immediately shakes his head, expression serious. "No, of course not. I was crazy about you."

That's what I thought too.

Then why did he break up with me?

"I was pretty smitten with you, too," I admit. Although he should've already been aware of where my heart was. I didn't hide how much I liked him back then, since he was my boyfriend.

He clears his throat, reaching over to rest his hand on top of mine. "I should've checked on you after I left and made sure you were okay…that you knew I didn't want to upset you. I'm sorry if my breaking it off the way I did and then leaving hurt you. It was the last thing I ever wanted when it came to me and you."

I take another bite, feeling more confused than ever.

If he didn't want to hurt me, he was crazy about me, and there wasn't somebody else, then why did we break up? I was ready to follow him to college or wherever his hockey career led him. I thought he wanted the same thing, but then it all changed one night, and before I knew it, he was gone. I was left behind, quietly nursing my tender heart, and swearing guys off for the foreseeable future. One thing it did motivate me to do was go to a college nearby and graduate. I put myself first and didn't think twice about another guy until after I graduated. Sure, I dated, but I never let any of them get serious during that time. Sean was always in the back of my mind anyway, so it was hard to let go of him easily.

"Thank you, I appreciate you saying that." I take my last bite and stand with my bowl. I set it in the sink, filling it with water, and grab the stuff for s'mores. I don't want to keep picking at an old wound, so I'm going to try and let it go. I don't want it to taint the rest of the night, especially when there's a possibility of a future for us.

I bring everything with me, setting the marshmallows, graham crackers, and chocolate bars on the table near the couch. We can make some later, once these heavy feelings have passed and the soup has had a chance to settle. The living room's still a bit cool, so the chocolate shouldn't melt before we want it to.

It's not long before Sean is doing the same, finishing his second bowl of soup, and coming to sit beside me on the mattress. We're close enough now that I lay my head against his arm and watch the blaze burn. I stretch my legs out, warming my toes closer to the toasty fire. The room may've warmed up a lot more, but the floors are still chilly from the lack of insulation.

He shocks me when he leans in and sweetly kisses the top of my head. Then again, as he places his hand on my thigh and gives it a firm but tender squeeze. My body buzzes all over for him, wishing he would touch me everywhere.

I sit up, shifting a bit to meet his gaze and say, "I wonder how long we'll be snowed in? If Pop will even make it out tomorrow with the tractor." The wind is blowing like crazy outside, and with all the snow, it makes me wonder if I'll get extra lucky and have Sean all to myself for longer than one night.

"I don't know, are you bored with me already?" He says it jokingly, but I can read the vulnerability in his expression.

I'm used to not having a TV or anything to entertain me except my family here, but Sean probably thinks it's weird and too quiet. I love it, though; the peace of this place is exactly what I needed after working so many hours and then coming to the farm and worrying over one thing after the other. The cabin has a way of taking away any outside distractions, and with us being snowed in for the time being, there's nothing I can do but take a mandatory relaxation day and soak in the time I now have off.

"Pretty sure I'm not the one we have to worry about getting bored. You're used to living an exciting life, probably spend a lot of time out and about in the city." I don't have to mention women, because we both know it's what I'm implying. But if he's going to be vulnerable, then I will be too.

He reaches for my hand, pulling it onto his lap, and not letting it go. We're close, basically arm to arm as we use the couch behind us to lean against. He stares at our hands for a moment before his gaze meets mine again. His brow furrows a bit as he claims, "I mean it, Winter. I never wanted to hurt you, and somehow…I know I did. The thought of it makes me feel terrible. You have to believe me when I say that the last thing I wanted was to leave you behind."

Tears crest, even though I try to fight them down. It's been years. This shouldn't still be bothering me like it does. My lip trembles as I finally find the nerve to ask the question I've always wondered about. I whisper, "Then why did you?"

CHAPTER SEVENTEEN

WINTER

    He glances away, releasing a deep exhale. His free hand moves for his hair, as he runs his fingers through the dark strands. He squeezes the back of his neck briefly before placing his hand back on his lap. His fingers tenderly stroke against mine while he's quiet for a beat. He eventually admits, "Because I was asked to."

    Now it's my turn for my brow to screw up with confusion. "What do you mean you were asked to? By whom?" His mom, maybe?

    "I promised I'd never say anything, and I'd never want to cause an issue, but we've lost so much time together, Winter." He shakes his head, staring deeply in my eyes, to the point I know he's serious. He's telling me the truth even though he's battling with himself over breaking his word to someone else. This man has a heart of gold, and somehow, I've always known as much; it's probably why I held on for so long. "I'm done losing my chances with you. Your grandfather approached me when we were dating. He knew about our plan to go to the same college."

I nod because I'd told everyone. I was beyond excited, and the fact that I had Sean by my side, I was on cloud nine, thinking our future together was solid.

"He confided in me that your family was worried you'd put your aspirations on hold for me, that my career would always overshadow anything you'd set your mind to, and you'd sacrifice too much for me."

"But that's what couples do for each other. It would have been my choice, just like it was when I decided to switch schools instead of ending up at the same college as you."

"No," he responds in all seriousness. "Not for me. I could never live with myself if I'd overshadowed or taken any of your hopes and dreams away. It would've ripped me in two if I'd found out once it was too late. I was torn up over your grandfather asking me to back off so you could 'forge your own path,' but I was also glad he'd been straight with me. I wanted you to have your chance, for you to do whatever your heart desired, so you'd be happy."

The tears that I'd been holding back a moment ago fall freely down my cheeks. Why does this hurt more than it did when he broke up with me all those years ago? Is it because my choice to choose him over everything else was taken away from me? College was great, I'm thankful I got my degree, but I could've and would've done all of that with Sean by my side as well. I can't believe that Pop, or the rest of my family, would do this. I understand why they did, because they love me and were looking out for what they believed was my best interest, but Sean could've been the love of my life, and that would've been taken from me before I ever had the chance to live my true happiness with another person.

With a sniffle, I murmur, "One thing I've learned in this life…You can have all the success in the world, accomplish everything you ever dreamed of, have the best of friends, the happiest of childhoods, but you know what? None of it would matter if you had to grow old all alone or without a person you love with every ounce of your soul."

I take a deep breath and then exhale as my gaze lands on our fingers, still intertwined together. I'm going to follow his lead and stop wasting time, too. He deserves to know what I think and how I feel. I meet his stare, saying, "I may not have known back then if you were the one for me, but it hurts learning the choice and chance of that sort of love with you was taken from me. I wasn't hopelessly in love with you back then, but I was already falling. A little more time together, and it would've happened for me. Believe it or not, Sean Spruce, but you're an easy man to love."

He offers me a soft, sad smile. "I would've loved you with every beat of my heart. I'm so sorry I wasn't honest with you about it back then. I was young and a little scared, if I'm being honest. I knew how close you were to your family. I couldn't say anything, especially when I thought I was doing the best thing I could for you, giving you your freedom to grow into your own pair of wings." He reaches up, his fingers tenderly wiping away my tears.

I lean in, resting my forehead against his. There's nothing I can do about the past and all the time we've lost, but it doesn't have to be our future. "You're a good man. Thank you for being honest with me now."

He nods and eventually lifts his head to press a kiss on my forehead. I sniffle a bit, allowing my tears to completely dry up while watching the logs burn down in the fireplace. Eventually, he gets up, adding more wood, and I grab our s'mores ingredients. We've had fun today, then a little bit of the heavy, so now it's time to enjoy some sweets and the time we get to spend together without any other distractions.

"I need chocolate," I announce and hop up. "The time has come; you're in for a new life experience."

He does a fist pump of excitement, making me laugh as I head into the kitchen to grab the thin metal sticks from on top of the refrigerator. As I'm reaching, I remember I was going to grab the space heater earlier, but got distracted. With the fireplace blazing, the old-fashioned wood-burning stove going, and the blankets covering everything, it's managed to keep the worst of the chill away, but I don't know if it'll be enough throughout the night. It also helps that I'm still wearing my fleece-lined leggings and sweater, since I was working in the barn earlier and needed to stay warm.

I set the heater up in the hall between the living room, where we're sleeping, and the bathroom. I definitely don't want to freeze my tush off in the middle of the night if I need a bathroom trip. I can't help myself and sneak glances at Sean as I do, with his striking jawline, five o'clock shadow, and high cheekbones. The man is ridiculously good-looking, and I'm finding it harder and harder to stop myself from staring like a weirdo. I manage to not trip over anything on my way back to the mattress, which is an accomplishment all on its own at this point, with how distracted I seem to be whenever this man is in the vicinity.

I toss the bag of unopened marshmallows at him, and it hits him on the side of the face. His hands scramble to grab it while laughing, since I caught him off guard for once. He immediately tears the plastic open and sticks his hand inside, grabbing one of the white fluffs of goodness to pop into his mouth.

"Oh my God, it's been so long since I've had one of these." He groans with delight, chewing, and then immediately places another in his mouth.

"That's cheating. You're supposed to roast them first," I say with a grin.

I steal the bag away and load two on my metal stick. He copies me when I hold the open bag in his direction again. He manages to swipe an extra, which he pops in his mouth, and so help me...as he chews, all I can think of is how delicious his kiss would taste right now.

"Your coach is going to put me on blast if he finds out about all the sugar I'm feeding you today. At your next practice or game, you'd better skate like it's Christmas Eve and you're Santa Claus."

He laughs, shaking his head at my comment. "Like Santa, huh?" His eyes sparkle, and I know he wants to say something else about my comment, but he's holding it back.

"What?"

"Have you been a good little girl this year?"

I snort and roll my eyes, "Please, buddy. There's nothing little about me, have you seen these thighs?"

I don't know why I say it, maybe because my guard is down and I'm having a good time. It doesn't even click what I've said until after I've already said it. Don't get me wrong, I love my curves. I've had them for my entire adult life, and have made peace that I'll never be stick thin, but still, I don't need to make Sean aware that I'm anything but confident. My thighs are a little bigger than I'd like, but that's a normal way to feel, even for those of us who've grown to love our bodies. I'm sure we all have at least one thing we'd like that was a little smaller, trimmer, or even thicker, curvier, longer, etc…

His big palm lands on my thigh, making me still in an instant. Heat fills me all over again with his touch. My cheeks are warm, and hello, it's not from the fire. One touch from this hockey stud has me zeroing in on where he's touching me, not able to think past how I want to put my hands on him, too. "I happen to think these thighs are pretty perfect," he pauses for a beat, then finishes, "For many things that I'd like to do."

I fan myself, suddenly wishing I was wearing a T-shirt instead of this knit sweater. I swear it's gotten hotter in here suddenly. "Are you, um, warm? Maybe we didn't need that heater on yet," I mumble, more to myself.

Sean's eyes sparkle with amusement, loving how flustered he easily gets me. We're not so young and innocent anymore. We're grown, and in this small cabin, all alone with nothing to do but keep each other company…Well, it has many different options running through my mind on how we can spend our time together.

"The temp's not bad. It's you, you're just hot." He compliments with a shrug.

My mouth pops open right about the same time the scent of burnt marshmallow fills the air. "Oh no!" I quickly scramble to grab both of our sticks and take them into the kitchen. Thankfully, the burning sugar on fire goes out with my quick jog to the kitchen, and then I'm grabbing a wad of paper towels to scrape the black goo off.

"Everything okay in there?"

"It's fine. Our marshmallows are burned beyond a crisp, though. We'll have to toast them again. This time, no distractions." I order, making him smile even wider. He's got a set of dimples on him that know exactly how to drive me wild.

"I can't help it if I'm smitten," he comments softly.

His admission makes me feel tingly all over. I'm so freaking smitten, too. He has no idea. I offer him his stick and two new fluffy balls of sweet goodness. "Okay, round two."

"That's what she said," he instantly responds, and then I'm shoving at his arm, playfully, while shaking my head. I like this side of him. Where the weight of the day no longer seems to weigh his shoulders down, and he's just sweet and easy to be around. It reminds me of why we became good friends in the first place and then later started dating. I didn't want our time together to end, so we made our relationship in to more.

This time around, we watch the marshmallows, waiting until they're toasty and soft to pull them free. I show him how I prefer to assemble mine, with double the amount of chocolate because I'm not about to skimp on my favorite part. My mouth waters as I lift my s'more toward my face, glancing at each side to decide on where I want to bite first.

"Mm, this looks so good," I practically moan the words, and then his head is suddenly in my way. He swiftly leans in and takes a giant bite out of my s'more. "Hey!" I yell in my chocolate outrage.

He chews quickly, swallowing the bite down, and then laughs loudly. I love the sound. Deep, rich, and every bit as sweet as the chocolate I was about to eat.

"It looked too good, I had to."

"Oh, it looked good, huh? Mine looked good enough to eat?" I grumble good-naturedly while fighting back a smile.

"Mmhm." He hums, then he quietly offers, "So good. Here, taste." He leans in again, but this time, *his lips land on mine.*

"Mm," I moan into the kiss. My free hand instantly moves to grip the front of his shirt, holding him to me, while his moves to cup the side of my face. In this moment, I know I'll never be able to get close enough. I want to crawl onto his lap, slip under his shirt, and burrow next to him for as long as I live. I drop the smore onto my lap and copy him, placing my other hand on his scruffy cheek.

He kisses me with everything he's got. Emotion and tenderness pour from him, and when our lips part, our tongues finally meeting, the taste of him mixed with smores explodes through my senses. Marshmallow, chocolate, graham cracker, and Sean…They consume my taste buds as the crackle of the fire and the soft pitter-patter of the snow falling in the background no longer reach my ears. I'm too far gone in the kiss, feeling everything he's giving me in the moment, along with everything I've missed over the years.

It was always supposed to be him, and now that he's finally kissing me, I can't seem to get enough.

CHAPTER EIGHTEEN

SEAN

I couldn't hold myself back from finally kissing her. With the sweet scent of roasted marshmallows in the air and candles she'd lit everywhere, snuggled under a blanket beside each other in front of the fireplace, there was no way I could resist Winter any longer. It turned into the most romantic, vulnerable moment we've shared, and when I made her laugh, I knew I had to taste her lips.

The kiss ended, and I sat here, my forehead lightly pressed to hers in awe. I can't stop staring at her, taking in every tiny detail on her face as I commit this moment to memory for the rest of my life. She's more special than I ever dreamed. I feel like when we were younger, it was just the tip of the iceberg. She's grown into such a wonderful, strong, smart, beautiful woman, and I'm counting my lucky stars I'm getting this moment with her right now. That she's willing to be vulnerable and show me she does still care about us means more than I can ever convey.

She finally breaks the silence as I'm busy counting every little freckle on her face. She whispers, "Promise me if it keeps snowing and we stay here for another night, we'll get the tree out of the truck and decorate it. Just the two of us."

I nod, sitting back. "I can't think of a better idea."

Glancing around the cabin, I take in the open floor space near one of the windows that would make the perfect spot to have a Christmas tree. I'm not sure if the tree we cut down will fit, but if not, I'll get her a smaller one without hesitation. We'll create our own Christmas memories together, which hopefully many years down the road we can look back on and cherish as a couple.

We finish our forgotten s'mores that ended up on our blanket, but were somehow still intact. My guess is the marshmallow was gooey enough to hold everything together; whatever the reason, I'm glad for it. They were delicious, and now I understand why Winter is such a fan. The fact that I got to taste her tongue when the time came to eat one only makes them that much more special in my opinion.

I hop up, place a few of the bigger logs on the fire, and tug my shirt off. I noticed her yawning earlier, so she must be worn out by now. "Ready to lie down?" I toss my shirt over the back of the couch, wondering if it's too soon for me to ask if she wants to sleep in it.

"Yes, but um, you have something..." she stands, pointing to my face. "Right here." She lifts her hand and I bend down so she can easily reach, since she's much shorter than I am. Rather than wipe whatever it is away, she presses a kiss to my cheek. Her tongue lightly licks the spot, and my brows jump. She has no idea what her licking me is going to do, and there will be no way for me to hide my reaction if she doesn't stop. She kisses the spot once more before backing up a step, "It was chocolate from my fingers. I couldn't let it go to waste."

I'm practically panting as desire cracks through me like a whip. "Right, chocolate," I mumble, breathless, as my heart beats double time. I normally don't sleep in my pants either, but removing them right now might not be the smartest thing. Especially if she decides to lick me again. It takes everything in me not to groan out loud with the enticing thought.

I fold the blankets down and shift the pillows around so she can crawl under them when she's ready. "Do you want the side closest to the fireplace since it'll die down some in the middle of the night? I sleep hot anyhow."

"Sure," she easily agrees. Her stare remains pinned on my naked chest as she pushes her leggings down to her ankles.

My lips part in surprise, my cheeks warm from the view of all her silky-smooth skin on display. My mouth waters for another reason entirely, the chocolate long forgotten with the sweet treat right in front of me. I try not to be rude and stare, but I also can't help myself as I watch her fold her leggings and then set them off to the side. She was worried about her thighs? I only see some sexy legs that are the perfect size for me to grip onto.

Next, she shifts around, moving her arms underneath her shirt. A moment later, and suddenly her bra appears in one hand, all the while she never even removed her shirt. I don't know how women can do that, but it's like magic watching it happen. She places the bra on top of her folded leggings and then turns to face me fully. I don't have to see every inch of her exposed; her curves are already on display with her pants missing and her shirt fitting her like a glove. There's still enough of a chill in the air to cause her nipples to pucker, and my groin tightens at the way her full, round breasts lie underneath the material.

Christ, she's sweet, sinful torture doing this to me right before I'm going to lie next to her. There's no way I'm going to be able to keep from getting hard while lying in bed beside her, knowing those tits are close enough for me to touch. I'm trying to be a gentleman here, but she's making it difficult enough for me that I probably won't get much sleep tonight. I'll be staring at the ceiling all night long, trying to think of whatever helps deflate an inconvenient hard-on. *Ice baths!* I can reminisce on how they feel from experience, and hopefully it'll be enough to put me to sleep.

She makes her way to the mattress, and as she sits, legs spread, I get a peek at her panties. They've got tiny sprigs of mistletoe and red bows printed all over them, and they're snug enough that I can see the outline of her fat little pussy lips. I'd never think of Christmas print underwear as sexy, but on her, I'm beginning to think I'll like everything. I lick my lips, unable to tear my gaze from her pussy until she's tucked underneath the quilts.

I turn to the side some, so she can't see how hard I am for her right now, and slide into bed. I'm silently thanking every good deed I ever did for giving me the reward of witnessing Winter without half of her clothes on. I know as soon as I close my eyes, I'll be picturing her completely naked, and it'll be impossible to sleep.

I clear my throat, finding it hard to formulate words at the moment when I'm so full of cum for her. "If you get cold, stay under the covers and wake me up, okay? I'll add more wood to the fire so you don't have to get up and freeze."

She turns toward me, gaze flicking between my eyes and my lips. I wonder if she'd be okay with me kissing her again? "Are you like this all the time?"

"Like what?" My breath catches as she shifts closer, her hands landing on me. One moves to my chest, while the other cups the side of my neck. If she comes any closer, I swear she'll find out just how happy I am to be lying beside her, and I'm trying to avoid that, not to put any pressure on her. I want her to be comfortable beside me and sleeping soundly tonight, if possible.

"Thoughtful. I think your love language is acts of service."

"Oh, yeah?"

She nods, leaning forward to press a soft kiss to my lips. When she pulls back, desire burns in her irises. She lies flat on her back, grabbing for my hands to pull me toward her. She sets them on her hips, and it hits me that her shirts no longer there. I shift my fingers higher, my palms gliding over her exposed skin, only to find she's pushed her shirt all the way up. My palms rest on her ribs, right underneath her breasts, and it's taking everything in me not to move them to brush against her breasts and accidentally graze those hard nipples I saw moments ago.

"Jesus," I groan, staring at her face, watching for any moment she may want me to stop. "Are you sure about this? I don't want you to feel pressured, or like I expect this because we're sharing a bed."

She reaches for my jeans, popping open the button. She lowers the zipper, reaching into my underwear and grabbing my cock as she admits, "I've dreamt of touching this cock." She pumps me roughly with her tight grip, making my hips shift forward and back. "Of sucking it into my mouth, and then feeling you deep inside me, filling and stretching my pussy, for a very long time. I want you, Sean. Only you. Please? Will you put me out of my misery here and finish taking my clothes off?"

"You're not the only one who's thought of my cock deep inside your pussy, of making love to you until you're full of my cum. In my case, it's been more times than I can count. If I take your clothes off, I'm going to want a taste from everywhere. I want my tongue in your pussy, in your booty, and all over your beautiful breasts. I want to lick every single inch of you, you know, to see which parts are the sweetest."

"Then by all means, have some dessert." She invites with a whisper as she watches me kick my pants off, then she moves my hand underneath her panties.

She's soaked, her underwear wet from her dripping slit. "Do you want my fingers inside of you first? Want me to fill your precious pussy and warm you up before shoving my big cock inside?" My fingers run through the wetness, loving how soaked my hand's getting from her excitement.

"God, yes," she whispers, her breath already choppy.

I pull my fingers free for a moment, sucking them in my mouth to taste her pussy juices for the first time. "Mm, so delicious," I comment, then push my hand back inside her panties. My fingers trail through her pussy lips, moving back and forth, nudging her clit a couple of times until she's writhing with need. Once I have her on the cusp, I press inside her entrance. She cries out with the motion, her pussy spasming like crazy as she climaxes, her pussy flooding my hand with her desire.

"So perfect," I compliment. "Are you sure this is what you want? We can stop right now, and I will still feel like the luckiest guy in the world."

"I'm more than sure," she shifts, shoving up her shirt until it's completely off, and she tosses to toward the couch. I tug her underwear off, and then we're both naked, lying beside each other and incredibly turned on. I've never wanted a woman so bad in my entire life before right now. "My pussy's all messy for you, you better clean it up."

"Mm," I hum with delight, and then I'm shifting below the blankets and between her thighs, desperate to show her just how much she means to me.

***

I'm suddenly woken up, pulled from a deep, sated sleep. I'd already woken up several times throughout the night to check on the fire, and each time I did, I also took the opportunity to pleasure Winter in a different way. I could've stayed up all night long, but after so many times of her shouting my name, while her thighs vibrated in satisfaction, I had to give her a break. And, after the last time, she'd drifted off, yawning because I'd worn her completely out. An intense feeling of satisfaction like no other filled my chest, and then I was out like a light, having the best dreams about the woman lying beside me.

I lift my head, glancing around the room, as I listen for what could've woken me up. The last log I put on the fire is about half the size it was initially, so I guess I could add another. I carefully shift my body away, trying not to wake up Winter, but that feat is nearly impossible as the noise I must've heard before becomes louder. I can't tell what it is, but the strange sound grows louder and louder. It's a cross between thump-thump and perhaps, whirring?

"Mm, what is that?" Winter sleepily grumbles.

"I don't know. I'm going to check," I whisper and get to my feet. The chill instantly hits my exposed skin as the blanket drops, and I no longer have our shared body heat to help keep me warm. We definitely need another log on the fire; it's way too chilly in here after all.

I hurry to the window as the sound becomes even louder, and I shove the quilt to the side. The window's frosted up too much to see out, so I hurry to the next. It's not as bad, thankfully, and I manage to see through the very middle of one of the panes. The light outside is at the weird stage where there's no sun, but you know it must be morning. It's overcast and dim, with white everywhere. I bet the kids in the village are taking full advantage of this, and there will be new snowmen built all through Tree Top Lane. It's rare we have a full-on blizzard before Christmas. Usually just some random snowfall, but maybe this was fate stepping in to give me another shot with Winter.

I glance at David's truck, noting how high the snow is on the side of the truck. It snowed *feet*, not inches. I'm guessing we'll be getting even more today with the way it looks outside. I know one thing for certain: I'm not going to be able to chop down another tree, so I'll have to try to unbury the one in the bed of the truck, and hope I can get enough of the snow off on the porch so it doesn't create a huge mess in the house later when Winter is ready to decorate.

As I'm staring out into the open area, my eyes widen in shock. "No way," I murmur, not believing what I'm seeing, as a helicopter slowly lowers to the ground.

"What is it?" Winter calls groggily, sitting up. She reaches over to the couch for her neat stack of discarded items and begins pulling her clothes on. While I hate seeing all of that perfect creamy skin being covered up, it's probably a good idea right now because I have no idea what's happening at the moment.

I follow her lead and hurry over to my discarded pile of clothes on the floor, tugging them on. "You're not going to believe this, but a helicopter just landed outside."

"Like on the farm? I hope my mom is okay!"

"No, a helicopter landed right in front of the cabin."

"You're joking…" She trails off, and I shake my head.

I race to the door, thinking there's only one person who would actually get a helicopter for me right now. However, I don't know how it's possible when no one knows my actual location. With that in mind, I'm just as confused and curious as Winter is at the moment.

Sure enough, a few minutes later, my agent, Spencer, jumps out of the helicopter. He's smiling widely as he attempts to make his way through the deep snow to the front door. He's not dressed for this weather. Which tells me he was probably picked up outside his office or somewhere just as warm, and then rode straight over here, keeping out of the brunt of the cold.

"Spencer?" I say by greeting, with my brows raised and an amused smirk lifting my lips.

"Spruce! My guy! How's it going?"

I quickly glance behind me, making sure Winter is indeed fully clothed, before meeting his stare again. "How did you find me?"

"I tracked your phone. I knew sharing our location with each other would come in handy one day. I'm glad it's only the snow getting in the way this time, and not you being gagged and kidnapped by some crazed fan. We got lucky." He replies in all seriousness.

With a huff, I point out. "It's early. I thought you wanted me to get some rest."

He nods. "I know, and we need to get out of here. I wouldn't have come if it wasn't important, so let's go."

"I can't just *leave*, I'm with someone."

"Well, champ, we have to. The chopper wasn't cheap, my friend, and time is running out." His brows raise as he silently implicates the important discussion we had yesterday about my future in hockey.

I sigh. Loudly. I know this is important. However, the last thing I want to do is leave Winter this soon after we shared our special night.

"We need to drop Winter off at her family's house before I can go anywhere else. I won't leave her here without my protection."

His eyes widen, "Winter?"

I nod. I'd briefly told him about her when he first became my agent. We were seeing a lot of each other back then since I was a rookie, and he'd asked why I wasn't married. I'd confided in him that there was only one woman I'd wanted to get serious with, but I'd let her go so she could forge her own future before I overtook it with mine.

"Her family owns the farm we're on, but her parents' house is a few miles away."

"Okay, yeah. Grab her and anything else you need. We'll drop her off first, then we can discuss the business that can't wait any longer."

I turn to let Winter know we've got a ride, but she's already there behind me, with her boots on and jacket in hand. "I heard him, Sean. We need to put the fire out before we can leave. I already unplugged the heater, and I can come back once the snow isn't so bad to put the blankets away and stuff."

"I'll help you," I offer, but she waves me off.

"Will you grab some snow to toss on the fireplace, please? You make sure that's out, and I'll put my jacket on. I can run around to the back to turn the generator off. It's easy, just a switch to flip."

"You got it." I press a tender kiss on her forehead and then move for the bucket next to the fireplace. I quickly tug on my jacket, then run outside to grab some snow. We don't have the time to wait around for the flames to die out on their own, so I grab a little to put the flames out, as I'm not trying to cause a melty mess. Once that's taken care of, I rush back outside in time to meet Winter as she comes around the side of the cabin.

"Fires out?"

"Yep, all taken care of." I grab her hand, tucking her close as we head for the helicopter.

SAPPHIRE KNIGHT

CHAPTER NINETEEN

SEAN

"Fancy," she comments, saying it in a posh voice. I know this must seem ridiculously over the top in her mind. Winter's always been the down-to-earth sort of girl, and it's something I appreciate more than ever. "You really are a hockey superstar, aren't you?" She flicks her gaze over me, "Well, la-tee-da. Sir Spruce."

I snort, chuckling, and shake my head. "Nah, I'm still just me. I have to review some contract stuff, though, so I'm guessing my agent thinks this absolutely can't wait." I kiss the top of her head, unable to hold back from touching her now that the walls we'd had up between us have come down.

Spencer opens the helicopter door, and I quickly grab it to help Winter inside first. I climb up next, closing the door behind me. Spencer leans over, making sure it's secured, while we buckle ourselves in. He hands us each a pair of bulky headphones to cover our ears with that have a microphone attached.

"Spencer, I'd like you to meet Winter. Winter, this is my agent, Spencer."

"Nice to meet you," they both respond.

Spencer gestures to the man beside him, who's in charge of all the important controls. "This is Chance, our pilot. He's a big hockey fan who was willing to do us a solid this morning and give us all a ride."

"Thanks, Chance. This is a pretty awesome helicopter you have here."

He nods. "Thanks, I wish I had one like this, but it's the company's that I work for. The partners at the firm in New York are big fans and season ticket holders, so they are more than happy to let me give you a lift. I'm honored to meet you, Spruce."

"The honors all mine," I respond earnestly, offering him a grateful smile. My time may've been interrupted by Winter, but it's not Chance's fault. He's just a fan doing a favor when he'd probably rather be home and out of this freezing weather.

"We'll be keeping low to help avoid some of the flurries and wind. The weather still seems to be a bit touch-and-go, but we should be in a clear pocket for about the next hour. This ride may get a little bumpy, but I assure you I will take all precautions. Does our next stop happen to be the house not far from here, the one with the big red barn?" He asks, beginning to flip switches, and then we're lifting off the ground.

I can't believe how big it is in here; we could comfortably fit another four people. Their firm must travel a lot for business to have this level of luxury and to be able to loan it out for a ride on quick notice. Spencer didn't just get us a helicopter ride; he practically got us a small plane with how secure and roomy it feels.

Winter confirms, "That's the one, my parents' house. Thank you."

We lift off fairly quickly, making my stomach drop at the sudden change. Winter grabs my hand for support, and it makes me feel ten feet tall. We're not up in the air for long; it seems like the flight takes maybe a total of three minutes tops, before we're lowering back down to the ground.

Chance gives Spencer the okay, and he opens the door. We get unbuckled from our safety belts, and then I climb out first. I hold out both of my hands for Winter, gripping her hips tightly to lift her to the ground. I don't release her right away, needing to feel her luscious curves against my bulk one more time before I have to leave her. I wrap my arms around her tightly, carrying her away from the helicopter.

She stares up at me, grinning as I walk. She's thoroughly amused I'm not letting her go yet. I murmur, "Thank you for yesterday. And for last night."

She blushes, nodding.

My fingers move to her chin, tipping her face up so she'll meet my gaze. "This is just business. I'll be back. And Winter? This thing between us is not finished. I want you in my life."

"Sean, I mean...*The helicopter*, and everything-" she gestures to the aircraft behind me.

As if I don't know how extra this is. Hockey players are known for being more on the low-key side when it comes to showboating, and this doesn't fit the mold. But neither does she. She's somehow more, and I don't know how to explain it, but my heart somehow already knows it.

"I know. Life can be overwhelming, but I promise this isn't a normal thing. I'll be back as soon as I can. Until then, stay warm and don't work yourself too hard." I glance up, noticing the mistletoe hung from the porch, nearly right above us. It was all over the cabin, too, but I'd ignored it in the face of being a gentleman. Now, however, I can't wait any longer, so I plant my lips on hers.

"Whoa! Simmer down now," is yelled from the porch, her dad's deep voice interrupting us.

I pull away, chuckling, and press one more kiss to the tip of her nose. The move makes her smile. "I'll see you soon. That's a promise." I repeat, and then nod to David. I swore to keep his daughter safe, and I've kept my word. I'm not about to shy away from kissing her now, so he needs to get used to seeing me treat her like she's my whole world, because she is.

"Be careful!" She calls as I take off into a jog back to the helicopter.

I wave, blow her a kiss, and then climb back inside. Spencer closes the door, meeting my gaze with his brows raised. I know he's probably got plenty of questions and opinions he's chomping at the bit to discuss, but he keeps them to himself for the moment.

We lift off as he's handing me a manila file folder full of papers. "You'll want to see these."

I open it, already expecting the folder to hold the offers that've been coming in from various teams he mentioned yesterday. Right on top is one from the Noelville Blizzards. The same team whose arena I've been using to train at while I'm home visiting Mom.

"What?" I ask with surprise. I had no idea that they were interested in me. I'm at their arena often to practice, and no one has mentioned anything. Not even in passing.

Spencer nods, flashing me a grin. "I know. There are several more, but when I saw that come through, I knew you'd want to see it as soon as possible."

"And the ride?" I question, having no idea where we're headed, only that I'm still in my clothes from yesterday, and I could use a shower. Maybe a gallon of coffee if we're being realistic. I peer out the side, watching the village pass below, and then we're heading toward Noelville. Or the airport. Or who knows with Spencer in charge at the moment. There's no telling what he's cooked up and has me agreeing to today.

"We have a meeting with their owner and GM in forty-five minutes. I figured it'd give you enough time to review the other offers and decide if you want to show up for our meeting or not."

I quietly flip through the various teams and what they're offering the Pines for my trade deal. This entire situation is out of the ordinary; you never hear about scandals like this in Hockey. In football? Yes. They're known for being problematic, with owners micromanaging everything and making terrible financial decisions. The potential bankruptcy and emergency trade deals with the Pines are going to be all anyone is talking about in the hockey world.

I'll be happy when all of the fuss dies down, and it's back to business as usual. I still can't believe the team and everyone are being so chill about working together to get everyone where they want to go. I need to find out what's happening with my buddy, Jake, and the rest of my teammates.

I glance through the other contracts, scanning the main points so I don't miss the most important things I care about. Spencer will have scoured them closely already, so he'll let me know the fine details on whichever option I decide to take. Two separate teams have three different players listed; they'd be willing to trade straight across to get me on their team. They probably believe they can make up the other two players' spots they'd be missing for cheaper than what the remaining balance is on my contract. Four teams are offering up a player, plus some cash. Their numbers aren't a full contract buyout, since they're offering a player in my place as well. Then, three teams are offering a full contract buyout.

Finally, there are the Noelville Blizzards and the Seattle Storm. Both teams are offering the Pines enough money to buy out my remaining contract, along with a contractual option of an extension for me, which I would have to agree to. I didn't consider that the teams might want me to sign on for longer; if anything, I was expecting the opposite and to be pushed into retirement.

We're landing in no time, it seems, since Noelville is so close to Noel Falls. I lean forward, saying, "Thanks, Chance. You have no idea what this ride means to me. Want me to sign anything for you or the partners you spoke of?"

"Do you mind if we get a selfie? My kids aren't going to believe this."

"Of course. Are they young?" He looks old enough to be my father, but I don't want to assume.

"No, they're older than you, I'm sure. My boys have been to several games, though, and to know I got some time with you without a crowd will have them running out to get their pilot's licenses."

We all laugh, and then I lean in, letting him snap a few selfies. Spencer helps out and climbs in the back to get a better photo of us, and then I autograph a few papers for him. We say our goodbyes and hop out.

"Take care, we'll be rooting for you!" He calls out as we wave and then closes the door.

Spencer and I hurry up the steps to the training facility since we were just dropped off in the nearest parking lot. Talk about a way to make an entrance. A few people stare, including some of the Blizzards showing up for morning skate. I wave, my cheeks warm from what they must be thinking is a total *divo* moment. I'm anything but a divo (aka man version of diva), and I pride myself on being laid back. I wonder if the GM or any of the other faculty saw us arrive as well.

"So, this option they offered. Contract buy-out with an extension agreement. What all does that entail? I was trying to read through each team before we landed, and I ran out of time. Does it mean what I think it does?"

"Walk with me," he says, and takes the folder. "Yes, they're willing to fork up the full amount of cash to buy your current contract out from the Pines. However, they want an addendum in place stating you'll consider an extension with them before you decide to retire or go to another team at the end of your term."

I open my mouth to speak, but he holds his hand up, so I'll wait, as he continues, "But that's not all. If you decide to retire or, God-forbid, are injured and can no longer play, they want you to consider a position on their faculty. Other teams also asked for you to consider a non-playing position with them if you decide to retire when this contract is up as well."

My mouth pops open. "Seriously?"

He nods, "You've hit new records this season. Which I'm guessing you haven't been paying attention to. You're easy to work with, players admire you, the media likes you…These really are your golden years, Spruce."

He claps me on the back, coming to a standstill, and asks, "Now what's it going to be? Do we climb into my rental?" He gestures to the black SUV he's no doubt had someone deliver here for him. "And, drive to the airport, to fly to another city and team? Or do we take the meeting here, and you end up getting exactly what you've been asking for?"

"I don't know how you pulled this one off, Spencer, but I only need two things. A massive cup of *strong* black coffee, and a pen to sign the new contract with the Blizzards."

He grins, clapping me on my shoulder. "That's what I thought, buddy, and it wasn't me. This is all you."

A moment later, a white sedan pulls up beside us. The window rolls down, and a bored-looking teenager pokes his head out. "You Spencer?"

"Yep, that's me." He steps next to the car.

"Pin?"

"Five-four-four-zero."

The kid nods, then hands over a tray with two large to-go cups and a bag. The scent of warm bread, sausage, and coffee permeates the air, assaulting my senses. I nearly groan as my stomach rumbles with hunger. Spencer slips him a twenty with his thanks, and then the kid drives off.

"This is why I pay you the big bucks," I comment as he hands me my cup. Steam escapes the opening as I take my first sip of the rich, bitter beverage. It works on warming me up instantly, and I'm no longer in a good mood. Now, I'm in a *really* good mood, on the cusp of breaking out in some celebratory Christmas carols that I'm sure Spencer wouldn't be impressed with. Winter, on the other hand, she'd sing with me.

The only thing that would make this day any better would be getting to spend it with the woman of my dreams. All while knowing that I'll finally be able to offer her a life with me, that she'll be happy living.

.

SAPPHIRE KNIGHT

Chapter Twenty

Winter

"Hmm," Dad grumbles as I pass him when I walk through the doorway. He reaches out with his good hand, giving my arm a squeeze of affection. He's a hugger, and being all broken, wrapped in casts, he can't do much. Poor guy. "Welcome home, looks like y'all managed not to get frostbite."

"Thanks, Dad, and nope, I'm fine. Good, even." The heat hits me as I step inside, and it makes me realize just how cold it truly is outside. He was right to tell us to stay put and not to try and make it back here on foot. I'd have been an icicle by the time we finally arrived.

"Hey, honey," Mom instantly greets, and wraps me in her embrace.

"Morning, Mom." I'm glad to see she's made it home safe and sound, but deep down, I knew she'd find a way. I know Dad must be relieved.

"What's all the ruckus? I'm watching my Hallmark Hunks in here!" Gram leans forward on the recliner in the living room, staring where we're all gathered in the entryway. She's got a knitted blanket over her lap, which she's tucked herself into, along with her crochet supplies. There are crocheted mini-dicks all over everything around her, probably for her book club later on in the week. My guess is the crazy woman has been up for a few hours already, dreaming up more ways she can traumatize her friends with. Last year, she spiked the cheese ball and brought bourbon pecan caramel candies. She didn't tell anyone they were full of liquor, and the next thing we knew, we were being called to give everyone rides home because none of the ladies could drive themselves anymore.

"A *helicopter*? What in God's name is that boy trying to prove?" Pop huffs from the entry to the kitchen. He sips from his cup full of coffee, frowning. His hair is pitched in every direction, telling me he's been running his hand through it like he does when he's thinking.

"Winter! I thought I heard something." Calla comes down the stairs wearing a wide smile. She's still in her pajamas, so she must've stayed the night in one of my siblings' rooms. Sean will be relieved to know she wasn't alone, I'm sure.

Apparently, I've come home to a full house. "Hi, everyone. Sean had an important meeting or something, so he dropped me off."

Calla's brow furrows, "The roads are all cleared? They were a mess last night when we got here." She moves to the nearest window, staring out at the white wonderland of snow surrounding the farm. Mom's SUV is out front, caked with muddy snow across the front, so they must've had a fun drive.

"Uh, no. He kind of flew off in a helicopter." I admit, watching as she and Mom grin at each other, thoroughly amused. "Dad, want to explain how Mom's SUV is parked in the driveway right now, when it wasn't plowed?" My eyes find him immediately, watching as he shrugs, looking anywhere but at me. He somehow managed to climb up in that freaking tractor to plow it for her! I know it, even though he won't admit as much.

Jesus, these people.

"A helicopter? Is that what I heard?" Gram questions, lighting up like this is the juiciest thing she's heard all week. "What a man!" She gushes, wide-eyed and grinning. "Frank! Bring me a coffee, and add that creamer I like so much."

She's talking about *Baileys*, not creamer. "Gram, it's a little early."

"Oh, bull. Early for you, maybe. Don't get snippy with me, missy, just because that beef stick dropped you off and didn't take you with him."

Pop grumbles to himself, going back into the kitchen, the scent of fresh biscuits hinting at the air. I bet there's a pot of sausage gravy on the stove, too, and the old man has been eating his weight in breakfast. If it were up to Gram and Mom, I'd have been walking down the aisle the same night I arrived, officially adding Calla to the family. These people are all nuts, but I love them, and surprisingly, I missed them yesterday. There's nothing like a freezing snowstorm to make you think of everything you value, and in this case, it's my family. Having Sean by my side didn't hurt things, as I find myself thinking about him every second of every day at this point. And last night…

Well, it was *perfect*. Beyond what I ever imagined it could be like between us, which is both thrilling and scary. He said he'll see me soon, and he's done nothing but prove I can trust in his word. However, there's still a small voice nagging in the back of my mind, reminding me to guard my heart until I'm absolutely certain I can give it away and not get it stomped on.

"Good morning to you all," I offer a tired smile. Sean had me up a lot last night, but you certainly won't hear a complaint out of me. The man kept his promise of keeping me warm, that's for sure. "I need a shower, then some coffee." I take off up the stairs before anyone has a chance to pepper me with any more questions. They won't get a peep from me, no matter how much they try to meddle.

I get to my bathroom just as a text comes through. I haven't had service since yesterday, but that's nothing new here. I plug my cell in as I swipe the screen to check it. *Could it be Sean already?*

Samantha: We'll be there tomorrow, if the weather lets us. If not, I may pull my hair out. I miss your face and need best friend time.

Samantha: I love these kids, but Josiah stuffed a cookie into one of the wall outlets and then smeared poo all across his bedroom floor last night. I tried cleaning it with toilet bowl cleaner, because hello, that's what it's for. I burned a huge spot in the carpet. Turns out that stuff really is strong. Josie hasn't stopped asking me if we can burn a J into her carpet next, and this morning, she climbed the counters to get her cereal before I was awake. Spilled three open boxes in the process.

Samantha: Send help.

Samantha: FML

I laugh. Loudly. Oh my God, I'd be pulling my hair out, too. Her kids are little angels. Every time I see them, I swear they're the cutest ever. They must be just as ready for a grandma visit as Samantha is. I set my phone back down, intending to reply after I've showered and my phone has had a chance to charge some.

Once the water warms up enough, I eagerly step under the strong spray, relishing in the steamy water. I scrub myself clean with my favorite peppermint body soap and wash my hair. After I finish rinsing and drying, I find my coziest, favorite sweater that's a bit well-worn because I wear it so often. I slip it on, along with some thick, fluffy socks, and a new pair of fleece-lined leggings. It feels good to be in clean clothes after taking a super-hot shower that nearly burned me in the process. I quickly blow-dry my hair and slather on some moisturizer, knowing I'm going to need it with the dry, wintery air.

I manage to slip into the kitchen and grab a to-go cup full of freshly brewed coffee. I add sugar, then pour in some sugar cookie-flavored creamer. The first sip hits the spot. It's not as good as my favorite cappuccino or hot cocoa from Tasty Sip, but it'll do the job.

"I'll be back after I check on the animals," I yell to my family and practically dash out the front door. Maybe if I stay busy long enough, they'll give up on the Sean inquisition. There's only one person I want to talk about Sean with right now, and that's Samantha. I need to call her so badly and tell her what happened between us, but I know we'll get our chance to dive into the details of everything tomorrow, so I'm going to wait.

I pull my phone free, remembering I didn't text her back earlier. Hopefully, she'll get my message before they arrive tomorrow. I'm sure all this crazy weather will only make our reception here worse, but after tomorrow, I won't have to worry since she'll be in town.

Me: Just got home, I was snowed in at the cabin. The main roads were supposed to get plowed, so hopefully it's clear for your trip. Text me when you get in town so we can meet up. I'm going to try and clear the driveway today with the tractor so I can get my car out. Also, FYI, Sean was at the cabin with me. I'll tell you when you get here.

Me: P.S. Your children are angels. They're ready to see grandma, so hurry up and pack!

There. I release a breath I was unknowingly holding while typing, and stick my phone in my pocket. Not a second later, it chimes.

Samantha: What?! Sean stayed with you? (shocked face emoji) I want all the details as soon as I drop the kids off at my mom's!

Me: It's a date. Now get in the car and start driving. Don't forget my holiday fudge.

It's my favorite. She stuffs it full of marshmallows, swirls it with peanut butter, and then tops it with some Christmas sprinkles. I don't know what else goes in it, but I'm pretty sure it's magic.

I check the barn first, making sure it's keeping the brunt of the cold out. I don't know what makes me glance up, but I do, and there's more mistletoe hung. *Who did this?* It wasn't Dad; the poor guy couldn't climb a ladder right now, no matter how hard he tried. It has to be Mom or Calla. They're the only ones who'd be up to something sneaky like this. Probably with the help of Gram, I'd bet.

Next, I check on the chickens, pigs, goats, and cows, making sure they get fed if needed, and also fill up their water if they're out. Some of it is frozen, so I spend time breaking it up and refilling what I can.

Afterwards, I grab one of the full gas cans and head for the tractor. I repeat the process two more times, making sure it has enough fuel. Then, I grab a few blankets from the barn since the tractor doesn't have heat, and I'm trying to make it through the day without freezing my tush completely off.

Hopefully, I can get enough of the snow cleared so I can make it back to the cabin tomorrow morning. I need to grab the boxes we left behind because the festival will be here before I know it. I can't do anything about Dad's truck until I find the spare and can change it out.

With a sigh, I glance around and silently wish again that Dasher were here to take care of everything for Dad. He's not, and won't be home for Christmas, so I do the only thing I can. I take a sip of my coffee and then climb up onto the tractor. It's time to get to work, and with the night I just had with Sean, it's enough to keep me distracted all day.

I can't wait for a repeat.

SAPPHIRE KNIGHT

Chapter Twenty-One

Winter

"Winter!" Samantha nearly screams with excitement as the door to the coffee shop closes behind her.

I wince at how loud she is, knowing we're drawing attention to ourselves. After the last debacle in here with my card declining in front of several people, I was trying to be low-key this trip. Lord knows how they like to wag their tongues, especially when my Gram is at the center of it all at times. I can't help but beam as I take her in. She's gorgeous, and I've missed her a ridiculous amount.

She's in her usual holiday attire, a sweater dress, black tights, and knee-high boots, with accessories to match the occasion. Her bracelet jingles since it's made out of bells; she's wearing a necklace with a single bell, but it's not cheesy. I'd bet it's platinum with real diamonds encrusted around the top, held by a long platinum chain. Her ears have matching diamond bell earrings that even I'd wear.

Did I mention her husband has a great job? Yep, my bestie gets spoiled, and her jewelry today is just one of the many that her husband likes to surprise her with. Although, after hearing about the shenanigans her kids put her through, I can see why he feels the need to spoil her with cute accessories. The man is lucky he has her.

"Gah, I've missed this. I've missed *you*!" I comment as I continue to squeeze her in a long hug. Every time I get to see her, I'm reminded how much time has passed between visits, and it makes me wish she lived closer.

"Me too." She tugs me with her to the counter, eager to order her favorite drink. "I'll take a large Cinnamon Gingerbread Cream Latte with whipped cream, and a spoonful of holiday spirit on top. I want one of those sugar plum danishes, too. Oh, and one of those orange cranberry pistachio muffins, please."

I just shake my head, watching as she oh's and ah's over everything in the case. This was me the first time I came back into town, too. I grab a sugar plum danish before we leave, since I already have my favorite cappuccino.

"Tell me about Sean." She demands immediately, already shuffling me outside. She waves and says hello to various people to not seem rude, but I'm not fooled. My best friend has one thing on her mind. "The deets, Winter, I need them. It's been *killing* me since you dropped that bomb of a text on me yesterday, and then didn't follow up with the good parts."

I can't help but laugh; she's always had a flair for the dramatics. Probably why Gram loves her so much, kindred spirits and all. "I'd say you had a pretty eventful day yourself, learning carpet design."

"Uh, don't remind me," she shoots me a mock glare, sipping from her coffee. "We are so not talking about my kids right this minute, when you finally got the D. It was good, wasn't it? I can tell already just from the way you're sparkling or whatever. Sean has a banger, and he dicked you down good."

"Samantha!" I whisper-yell, slashing my hand across my neck in the universal language of shut the heck up.

"What?" She glances around, claiming, "No one will hear us. That's why I had us come outside." She taps the side of her head, "Already thought of the coffee shop gossipers."

I nod, feeling the fluttering sensation of nerves and excitement swirling around in my stomach as I think of my time with Sean. "Yes, it happened, and I can't stop thinking about him no matter what I do. But, that's not all."

She squeals in delight, doing an excited shimmy, making me grin. "It's not? What else have you not told me about?"

"He's been coming around the farm ever since I first got into town. I drove off the side of the road at the bottom of the mountain on my way here. I must've hit ice somewhere, then I slid to the side, and my car was stuck. I was stranded on the shoulder when he offered me a ride."

"No way, that sucks. Twenty-eighteen all over again."

I nod, "Tell me about it. I was having flashbacks for sure. Anyhow, after that, he and his mom spent Thanksgiving with us, and he's also been helping with festival stuff...There's been a lot of buildup, so it wasn't just a night at the cabin. He promised my dad he'd keep me safe, and he took it *so* seriously. I don't know what to say, aside from admitting that he's stealing my heart."

She gasps, "Yes! This makes me super happy for you. It's about freaking time Sean Spruce pulls his head out of his skates and realizes he can't live without you."

Laughing, I try to downplay it, but her words do hit home. "He's a good guy, and he's been doing just fine living without me." I finally take a bite of my danish. It's heavenly, but they're small. Three big bites and I have it finished, only the sugar left behind on my fingers as any evidence.

"You sell yourself short, Winter, but that's not an issue anymore because now he knows how amazing you are. You two are going to spend forever together, I already know it."

"How can you be so sure?"

"Because he used to look at you like you were his favorite thing besides hockey. I can only imagine how badly he's fallen for you this time around."

We're interrupted by the Goldsteins, who own the local grocery store. "Hello, girls!" Mrs. Goldstein greets with a welcoming smile as she and her husband stroll by. They've gone for a daily walk together, usually holding hands through the village, for as long as I can remember.

"Hello," We echo, watching the old couple amble by.

They're tucked close together, slowly making their way down the sidewalk that's been freshly scraped and salted by the various businesses lining the road. They point out and appreciate the various cheerful holiday decorations as they go. Gum Drop Lane is always a sight to see, with tons of lights adorning every storefront's windows. A few shops set up actual holiday scenes in the windows as well. The small toy store at the end of the block does one of my favorites, with an electric train circling a Christmas tree that's been decorated in small nostalgic toys as ornaments.

Thankfully, the roads are also seemingly much better today, so people can get where they need to be once again. We've had snowstorms my entire life, so it's not something the people around here worry too much over. The roads always end up cleared, including the mountain coming in and out of town, so we just roll with it as much as we can. The resilience we show as a community is something everyone should be proud of, I think. Everyone always leans in and offers a helping hand whenever possible. Including opening up our homes if a neighbor needs it. Somehow, everything always ends up working out.

The chime from Tasty Sip's glass door rings behind us. The bells momentarily mixed with a blast of warm air and Christmas music playing, from someone leaving the coffee shop. It's enough to break our illusion of privacy and get us moving down the sidewalk.

"When are you going to see him again?" Samantha asks as we head in the direction of Sandies Boutique.

I still need to pick up a few gifts, and thanks to my money being returned to my bank account, I can finally finish checking everyone off my list. I shrug, "I don't know. He said he'd get a hold of me. His agent showed up, and I managed to catch snippets of his conversation he'd had with him the day prior. I think something's going on with Sean's contract."

"Seriously?" She meets my gaze, hers filled with curiosity. I know she wants to probe for more, but I don't have much to offer, unfortunately.

"Mmhm." I open the door to Sandie's Boutique, holding it for her to enter before me. "Which is another reason why I don't want to get my hopes up too high."

We're interrupted by the owner, "Hello, welcome in." It sounds pretty standard for a greeting, but then she does a double-take, and her tone shifts completely. "Oh, Winter and Samantha! Look at you two. I swear, you should enter *Miss Noel Falls Christmas* this year. I have the absolute perfect dresses for the occasion. You just let me know and they're all yours."

"Thanks, Sandie." I kindly reply, knowing darn well there's absolutely no way I'm entering to be Noel Falls' Miss Christmas.

Samantha won't either. I'd bet she'd rather eat cookies made with too much salt instead of sugar than enter that contest and be forced to ride in the parade on Christmas Eve, while doing her princess wave. She's terrible at waving. There's no way she'd pass the vibe check and would end up chunking candy canes at someone's face. It'd get published in the paper, and then the town would vote to never let her enter another holiday contest again. It'd turn dramatic, fast, and I refuse to allow my best friend to go down in a blaze without me.

"Your hopes need to be up where Sean is concerned. You'd better expect him to fully commit, or I'm hunting him down and dying all his clothes Pepto-Bismol pink. I'll do it, we all know how bad I am at laundry." She whispers the threat, with a determined nod.

I shoot her a strong, wide-eyed look, attempting to silently convey that she needs to stop talking about it. Sandie is a sweet lady, but she won't hesitate to spread some juicy news the first chance she has at the church bake sale this Sunday.

I mumble, "I'm not expecting anything. Just going with the flow." It's not completely the truth, but I'm sticking to it anyway until I'm proven otherwise.

Sandie blindsides me, coming out of nowhere. She holds a bright red dress with far too much mesh fluff stuff underneath the skirt, directly in front of my face. "How's this?"

"Oh!" My hand flies to my chest as we both jump in surprise. *Jesus H. Christ!* The woman nearly had me slamming into Samantha. She's like a little old holiday ninja elf.

"Where did she even come from? I nearly shat my pants!" Samatha gasps in shock from behind me, and it takes every bit of my self-control I possess to keep from bursting out laughing.

Sandie pops over to another rack before returning with two matching ugly dresses, one in holiday green, the other in dark blue. "They'd be perfect for the contest, or even a date. Surely, you'll be at the Jingle Bell Swing?" Her excitement grows as she continues, "With a date? I heard that handsome Sean Spruce dropped your car off at the shop to get fixed, and his truck's been seen at your family's farm every time he's in town."

I back up a step as I realize I should've waited longer before coming in here. "Um, the Jingle Bell Swing?" How did I forget about the dance? It's put on every year, and used to be one of my favorite activities that the village organizes.

Probably because I've been too worried about getting everything ready for the festival. Then, toss Sean into the mix, and suddenly, I only possess two brain cells, it seems. There's no way I'm going to have time to make it to the dance on top of everything else.

"We'll stop by." I automatically agree for me and Samantha both, before I manage to shut my trap and stop over-committing myself. "But it all depends on whether I can get everything ready for the festival in time. You know Dad's been hurt, and Mom's busy, so that leaves me trying to prepare."

She nods, sympathy softening her expression. "Oh, you poor sweet girl. You don't worry yourself about the dance. I'll have dresses in stock if you can get the time off to go; if not, I'll be stopping by your booth at the festival. Your family's candies are my favorite sweet treat to have in the store for my customers."

"Thank you, Sandie, that means a lot."

I end up grabbing one of the cute belts like Calla had on, and then I pick out a few more gifts. We pay for our purchases, and then I quickly tug my best friend outside as soon as possible. Any more time and we may be coaxed into buying dresses we don't need. For any occasion.

"I wonder who we'll see at the dance wearing those dresses?" She ponders as soon as we're walking back down the sidewalk.

Laughing, I shake my head. "I don't know, but someone will post it on social media for sure. Sandie is so sweet, but she nearly gave me a heart attack, thrusting all those sequins in my face. Then there was the mesh."

"So. Much. Mesh."

I nearly finish off my drink, debating stopping by Tasty Sip again for a refill. I wonder what Sean's doing right now? Would it seem too needy if I texted him to ask how his day's going? Probably. I suck at this relationship stuff; it's partly why I never really try to have a full-time boyfriend. "Should I text him?" I mutter, glancing around. I wish he'd pull up right now, like he's been randomly doing since I got into town.

"Oh my God!" Samantha shouts suddenly, making me twist toward her in a panic.

"What?"

"I can't believe I didn't realize this as soon as you said something, but I know what's going on with Sean. It's all over the news!"

I stop walking, needing her to spill everything she knows. "Wait. You do? What is it?"

"The Pines are going bankrupt. They have to trade off their most expensive players to try and recoup enough money to keep them in the league. They were talking about it on the radio on our way here, too."

Dad's comments about Sean's latest contract come back to me, reminding me that he said it was more than other players were getting. My gut tightens with apprehension, my hand clenching tighter around my shopping bags. I take a sip of my cappuccino, which usually fills me with holly jolly spirit like it's supposed to, but this time, it just tastes like too much sugar. The realization of what this means for Sean has everything around me feeling a lot less colorful and cheery.

"Sean's getting traded," I quietly utter the words. My lower lip trembles, while tears start to swim across my vision at the realization of what this means. The impact hits my heart like an avalanche, making me stumble.

Samantha catches me, wrapping her arm around my back. She hugs me from the side as a quiet whimper of sadness leaves me. "I'm sorry, my friend," she says softly, then echoes, "Sean's getting traded."

He'll be too far away before we ever get a chance to have our happily ever after.

Chapter Twenty-Two

SEAN

It's been nearly a week since the last time I saw Winter, but I can't help it. After the meeting with my new GM and the Blizzard's team owner, I had to fly straight to New York with Spencer to meet with the Pines and let them know which deal I wanted them to accept on my behalf. I also owed it to my teammates to go out and have a proper goodbye with them since the change came on so suddenly. Some of those guys I've known since I was as young as fifteen, and I'll miss seeing them daily during the season. Our night out was filled with darts, pool, and a lot of ribbing each other and laughs.

I'll especially miss my closest friend, Jake. In my meeting with the Blizzards, I'd mentioned in passing about them trading for him, too. I tried to sell it as us being a powerful duo for the Blizzards' season if they were to send in an offer for him, too. I was hoping I could feel them out a bit and see if they had any interest in him...However, they wouldn't offer up any details to me, just that they'd keep him in mind.

Of course, the moment I saw Jake, I basically bombarded him with trade questions. I'd asked about the possibility of him moving teams with me, because not only would I feel more comfortable having him walk onto a new team with me at the same time, but we'd also get to be close to each other on our off time. I've gotten used to having him around and would like to keep my closest buddy around if possible. He let it slip that the Blizzards are in talks with his agent, but he doesn't have any offer details yet. I'm hoping the deal pulls through and he ends up on the same team.

I won't deny it, leaving the Pines is one of the hardest things I've had to face as an adult. I've been a part of their organization since I was a kid, it seems. When they signed me, they made me one of the faces of their franchise, and I'll never forget the unwavering support they've shown this entire time. I always thought I'd end up retiring a Pine, and the realization that my life is taking a different toll is both exciting and frightening. We've merely scratched the surface on our season so far this year, and now it feels like the work I put in for them already has been a waste of my time. They should've let us go before the games started, so we could've started with our teams from the beginning. I'm going to go out on a limb here and speculate they were trying to rake in as much cash as possible by having us on their roster, and it still wasn't enough to climb out of the hole they've dug themselves into.

Now, I have to get accustomed to a new team and their dynamics basically as fast as I possibly can, so we don't mess up our games and end up with a losing streak. I know a few of the guys on the Blizzards, which is pretty common when you've been playing in the league for as long as I have. You get used to meeting people traveling back and forth, plus all the different types of games they can call you up to play. Charities, the Juniors, college, you name it, and we're expected to play with whoever they throw us together with. George, the Blizzard's owner, seems a bit overly excited that I've agreed to their terms, including the extension and the after-pro retirement options they've offered. He mentioned following my career since I was in the junior league, which I took as a huge compliment. It's always a good feeling when you know someone is a fan, especially a team owner, and not only because I've held some records throughout my career.

Grabbing my belongings from my old training facility was bittersweet; knowing it'll never be my locker space again hit a little harder than I was anticipating. Packing my other stuff up to move didn't take much time or effort. I'd leased a fully furnished apartment in New York, so my stuff there mostly consisted of clothes. I mailed a few boxes to Mom's house until I figure out my new living arrangements. That's another wrench to toss in and shake things up, me jumping into house hunting mid-season.

I probably can't live in Noel Falls because of the unpredictable snowfall on the mountains surrounding the village, but I could be close. Very close. And, as I've gotten older, I've come to realize it's what I've been wanting in my life. Being nearby, just in case Mom needs me.

Now, I have Winter to think of too... Well, hopefully anyway. I'm over here crossing my fingers, toes, and everything else I possibly can that she'll want a future with me because I don't want to live the rest of my life without her in it. My working in Noelville gives me a sense of newfound courage where she's concerned, and I'm confident in asking her to stay this time...

For me.

Us.

Gah, she's the only woman I can picture my future with. If she's not ready, it'll crush me.

It's been a whirlwind of a few days attempting to handle everything as quickly as I can, and get back so I can play in the next game. The Blizzards didn't take over my contract to give me time off and to watch me sit on the bench. They'll want to get their money's worth out of me playing, I'm sure. I stayed at a hotel last night next to the airport, knowing I had to be here early for our morning skate.

I finally sent Winter a text letting her know I'll be back in town soon, but it wasn't enough. At least not on my end, I want to hear her voice because I've missed her. Even if it hasn't been a full week, at this point, any amount of time away from her is too long in my book.

"Spruce!" One of the janitors greets me as I enter through the players' entrance at the back of the arena.

The Blizzards don't have a separate facility like the Pines do, but maybe that's also why this team could afford to step in so quickly and take over my contract, whereas the other one is nearly bankrupt. My head is still spinning over the news. How could they blindside everyone like this? They have so many people, and not only the players who are depending on them. I feel bad for anyone they lay off, and I'm no longer there to try and do anything about it either.

"Hey, how's it going?" I ask the older gentleman.

He looks like he could be someone's grandpa, reminding me of Santa Claus. He's whistling a Christmas carol as he works, so he must enjoy his job here. I slow my pace enough not to come off as rude, even though I need to get to the locker room and gear up. I don't want to be the last guy in the room on my first day to work; it wouldn't set a shining example.

"Better now that we have you in a Blizzard's jersey!" He smiles, and I return his enthusiasm with a grin of my own.

"Thanks, that means a lot. I'm excited to be a part of the team." I bump his knuckles with mine as I pass him. "Have a good day, man."

"You too, and welcome to the home team. You'll find a lot of people are very happy you're here." He mentions and turns away. He dusts off a few of the team's ornaments and then replaces them on a Christmas tree that's been set up next to a water fountain. I don't miss two that have my name on them. How they've gotten ornaments for me here already is beyond me, but it's seeming more and more as each minute passes that I'm meant to be here.

I've practiced in these facilities many times when I've been home visiting, with special permission, of course. I came in even if it was just to get some skate time in, so I'd always be ready for the next game. However, I've always entered through the front entrance in the past with the assistance of an employee, and while everyone has been polite, it was never as friendly as the janitor was moments ago. I'm taking it as a good sign of what's to come, being accepted here even though I've been an opponent in the past.

I pull the bright red door open that leads to the team's locker room and make my way down the short hallway. As I round the corner, I'm greeted with cheers. The grin I was just sporting out in the hallway morphs into a wide smile. Everyone's on their feet, clapping and shouting my name, welcoming me. As a couple of the guys shift to the side, I find the familiar face of the player I was going to miss the most from the Pines.

"Jake?" My eyes are wide, my mouth dropping open in surprise.

"I'm here!" He grins, and then we're bro-hugging our excitement out. "They signed me, Spruce. I caught the red eye to make it in before you arrived. No way was I missing your face when you walked in that door for the first time. You're never gonna live down the excitement I just witnessed," he threatens with a laugh. "We're Blizzards, baby!" He yells.

I'm laughing as I release him; my energy is already bursting through me, making me ready to get out on the ice and skate to burn some of it up. Turning to the others, I immediately start shaking everyone's hands. It's important that they know I'm committed to all of them as well, and having Jake around is one hell of a bonus for me. Not to mention he's a very talented player, who whom I work well with, so they're getting something out of our friendship as well.

"Thanks, everyone. I appreciate the welcome. It's great to see you guys, and also to meet some of you for the first time. Especially while we're not playing against each other." They chuckle, and a few I already know step forward to offer me a bro hug, welcoming me to the team.

"You couldn't have come at a better time," McGregor says and steps forward, clapping me on my back. "You know our captain was injured badly at the start of the season, and we've received an update from the team doctor and owner. They made it official that he's not going to be able to return. You have no idea how happy we are to see this trade happen, Spruce. We need you to step in and fill that role we're missing."

"Oh no, that sucks. I'm sorry to hear that." His words don't hit me at first; I'm momentarily distracted by worrying we're down a strong player for the rest of the season.

He nods. "It's career-ending ending and while we all love the guy and will miss him, when we found out about the trade, we took it as a sign. We need a captain to fill his spot, and now you're here."

I'd been moving to my locker, but my steps falter with the weight of his words. "Wait, what?" I ask, flashing my gaze around the room. Several guys have been here for years, so I must've heard him incorrectly. I just got here, and some of these players I'm meeting on good terms for the first time. Hell, a couple I could probably be their father, it seems, with their fresh baby faces staring at me.

"Yeah. We talked about it, and none of us is ready for that type of responsibility, or we don't want it. Especially with someone like you coming on the team, with all of your experience. Every single one of us looks up to you. We're getting the chance to play beside a hockey legend. We took it to Coach and our GM last night, and they agreed with us. You deserve to wear the C. To start your career here the right way."

"But I haven't earned it with you all."

Checzok steps forward, lightly smacking my shoulder as he says in his thick Russian accent, "You will. We believe in you. Lead us, man. You've earned this with your career." He gestures to the brand-new practice jersey hanging in my locker, and I notice straight away that it already has the captain's patch sewn in place.

They're completely serious about this.

I swallow, feeling a bit choked up. Not only is it an honor that the team and upper management would consider me fit enough to be their team captain, but it's a lot of added pressure. I'll get a lot of clout if we win, but if we lose, well, it'll be my fault too.

"Speech!" A young player named Johnson chants a few times, making our teammates laugh and join in.

"I don't have a speech; in fact, you guys have made me go mute," I admit, shaking my head. This means more than I can express; it's something I didn't think I'd be rewarded with in my career.

"You stole the words from him, fellows, be shocked!" Jake shouts, and then everyone is laughing and giving me a bit of ribbing. I'm jostled around as affectionately as a bunch of rough hockey players can manage.

Raising my hands, I say, "I'm honored. But, *if I'm going to be your captain*, then there's only one thing I need to be saying right now. Let's get out on the ice, boys, it's our time!"

"Couldn't have said it any better, Spruce," My new coach says from the doorway and offers an encouraging nod. The guys cheer and shout, amping each other up, then we're all hustling out to the rink once we've finished lacing up and taping our skates.

I take in the arena, my new home away from home. It's decorated for the holidays right now, but I'm not looking at them, no, I'm staring at the banners hung from the ceiling. I know it then and there; I'm going to give this team the best years of my career. I'm going to put a banner up there that when the fans look up, they remember my time and dedication here. They'll remember how I came in and made this a team of champions once again, that they can be proud of.

My blades slice across the fresh ice, and as the cold air of the rink hits me full force, everything feels right. No, it's better, in fact. If I can get Winter to agree to stay with me, then every one of my Christmas wishes will be coming true this year. A feat I never thought I'd see happen, but here I am.

We run drills, getting ready for the next game, and I'm pleased to find that I instantly gel with a few of the other players. I've been studying everything I can about the team in between my packing and moving, ever since I signed my new contract. I'm vibrating with excitement to put on the new jersey, play in the next game, and see how everything turns out. I have a great feeling about this team and this season, because with me wearing the captain's patch, I'm going to do everything in my power to make sure we're a playoff team.

Champions.

Marrying Winter and winning the Stanley Cup are the next two things left on my list to accomplish. I hope these guys are ready to work, because motivation like I haven't felt since I was a rookie is right underneath my skin, pushing me forward. As I slam a puck into the net, all I can think about is how excited I am to tell her all about the new team and my move.

Jake slides to a stop beside me, his hand landing on my shoulder. "Patch looks good on you."

I nod, "Thanks. Means a lot coming from you. And that you took whatever they offered you to be here. It would be weird doing all this without you here."

"Aw, man, they were good to me. I'm happy, plus they opted for a possible extension when my time is up. They want to keep us playing together if they can afford it. So, what's next? You're back home, you have the team behind you, and a woman right down the road. Are you seriously going to hang around here all day and not go see her?"

I meet his stare, shaking my head, because no way am I not going to go see my woman. "What about you? Do you have someplace to stay?"

He shrugs, waving my question off like it's no big deal. "I got a room at the hotel down the road."

It's the holidays, and he's my best friend; he's not staying at a hotel if I can help it. "No way, you can stay at my mom's. She won't mind. She's always asking me about you anyway."

He wiggles his brows, "Moms love me."

I smack his chest with the back of my hand. "Shut up, bro."

His loud laugh follows me as I skate to the edge of the rink and head for the locker room to shower and change. It's time I saw the woman I can't seem to get off my mind, and let her know just how serious I am when it comes to me and her.

Chapter Twenty-Three

Winter

I'm set up for the week of the holiday festival, and my booth is looking a little sparse compared to what I'm used to. It's okay, though. I have time to make more gift baskets and candies each day before I have to be here, so that will help some. Mom and Calla have helped me decorate, since Samantha is on kid duty. Her daughter has come down with something, and she's hoping it's just a bug and goes away quickly. I swear, being sick during the holidays is the worst, especially around here when there are so many activities planned for the community.

I wave as a few little kids run through the designated walkways, calling hello. They must be in kindergarten by now. I went to school with their parents, and now it's surreal to see those same people having children of their own. It makes me feel like I'm behind schedule somehow. When I'm in the city, I don't notice it as much because there are more people my age without kids, busy working and having fun with friends. Here, it just makes me realize what else I'm missing out on.

A shiver wracks through me as I watch everyone stroll by. It's cooled down more today since it's gotten dark out, and I'm sure I'm not the only one feeling it. With all the twinkling lights and mini-Edison bulb stands strung everywhere, it's turned the park that we've all set our booths up into something out of a fairytale. There's a tent in the center with heaters, large wood picnic tables, and chairs so people can get warmed up while eating their food and treats they've bought from various vendors, and visit with friends. The festival is always held here because it's right next to the small ice rink that the chamber of commerce sponsors each year.

I rub my hands together, blowing between them. I have gloves on, but my hands always get cold regardless, and I'm hoping the friction might give me a bit more warmth. The chill has taken over, despite the festive atmosphere around me. Our farm's little booth is positioned near the edge of the park, giving me a perfect view of families bundled up in their festive scarves and mittens as they wander from one vendor to the next.

The location is also close enough to the pop-up rink that all skaters pass by when they head for the benches to take a break. Thankfully, it's not too close that I'm constantly hit with the spray of ice when someone stops too quickly, because that would surely take all the jolliness I've managed to muster right out of me. I can't help but watch as a couple of families glide across the ice, their laughter creating puffs of white in the frosty night air.

Everyone seems happy, making me think back to the time Sean had taken me skating for one of our dates. I knew how to skate already, having lived here my entire life. For his sake, I pretended to be rusty so he'd have a reason to help me.

I shake my head with a chuckle. I was young and thought I had everything all figured out. Turns out I had no idea what life entailed for me, or the second chances it'd offer.

Speaking of Sean...

I pull my phone from my pocket and reread his text for like the fifth time that says he'll be seeing me soon. However, he hasn't shown up yet. I know he's a busy guy, so I haven't texted him, but it's been hard not to. I don't want to come off as clingy or anything; the man hasn't made me any promises. Nor have I asked him to, but it still has me hoping that in the end, he'll want to be with me as much as I want to be with him.

Gram makes her way into the booth alongside Mom and Calla. "Hot cocoa?" She holds out a large cup, and I can already see the steam escaping from the opening in the lid.

"Absolutely, thank you."

The owner of Tasty Sip first started her business at these markets, and it wasn't long before it blossomed into her shop on the main street. I carefully take the first drink, expecting it to be hot. Instead, I get a little bit of hot cocoa and a lot of whipped cream and marshmallows. Sweetness explodes over my tongue, instantly making me swallow and laugh a little to myself.

"So good. I swear she sprinkles Christmas dust in her drinks to make them so good." I mutter.

Mom smiles, nodding. "Even the flavored hot coffees she serves are the best around. I'm so glad to see their booth set up again this year. I was worried the shop would be too busy, we'd be out of our favorite drinks while we're here."

Gram sits in her chair in the corner, bundling up in her newest quilt. "The only thing I'm looking forward to is the eye candy. I can't wait until the ax-throwing contest, and we've got prime seating this year." She nods to the setup that's been roped off beside the rink, and is filled with various logs and ribbons already tied off for various markers.

I roll my eyes. The woman is crazy. I don't know how Pops puts up with her. She's been feisty like this for as long as I can remember. "Tomorrow, Gram. They only do ax-throwing when it's light outside."

"And with good reason, too. We need all those glorious muscles on display," she offers me a wink.

Mom and Calla laugh and turn away to talk to various people stopping by the booth. In this town, we know everyone, and they all want to say hi to Mom since she's their doctor and Calla's their nurse. I keep smiling and waving to each of them so they don't think I'm being rude or unsociable, but in reality, I only want to see two people today, and neither are here. Sean and Samantha.

"I swear those roasted nuts have had my mouth watering ever since I got here." I groan a moment later as my stomach rumbles. They coat them in this cinnamon and sugar concoction, along with who knows what else, but it's the only time I randomly eat a bag of nuts like that.

"That's what she said!" Gram comments, grinning.

Mom flashes her a wide-eyed look, "Mom! Not so loud, *please*." She's Dad's mom, but my parents have been married for like thirty-five years, so at this point she calls Gram *'Mom'* too. If Dad were here, he'd be turning red, not able to wrangle Gram in. It's always entertaining to see him try to handle her, and Gram reminds him she'll say or do whatever she wants.

"Well, look who finally showed up. Guess he left the helicopter at home this time," Gram nods a beat later, her head tilted in the opposite direction that I was just staring off in.

I try to act nonchalant when turning to look, but I'm not sure if I pull it off or not. However, as soon as my gaze falls on Sean, everything inside me lights up. I'm excited to see him, and not only that, but *I missed him*. He's striding through the festival, another big guy at his side as they talk and laugh together. I've watched enough games to know it's his good friend, Jake. It's not the man's presence beside him that takes me most by surprise; it's the fact that they're both wearing thick hoodies advertising the Noelville Blizzards hockey team.

A few people stop them to excitedly shake their hands, saying hello. Some teens race up to the two of them, hands full of napkins, with a couple of red and green markers they've swiped from the kids' craft tables. I have no doubt they're asking for autographs.

The guys sign several items, wearing smiles as they do it and I can only imagine how crazy their lives must be on game days with people rushing to see them. I'm captivated by the entire scene; I've never been around Sean when he's been anything more than just 'that good hockey player I know' who people would randomly compliment on in the village. Now, however, he has legit celebrity status, and it's intriguing. He goes with the flow so well and seems genuinely happy to autograph stuff for people.

The teenagers ask the guys something, then they both nod and turn around. I zero in on the back of their hoodies, as I notice that it has each of their last names and numbers in large print. When the realization of what it means hits me, my mouth drops open.

"You see what I am, or have my eyes gotten worse?" Gram nudges me, but I'm not paying her any attention. The woman can see just fine; she's not fooling me.

Calla gasps, quietly whispering, "Oh, please be true!"

I know she's wishing the same thing I am, but for different reasons. Sean's been living away from Noel Falls for a long time because of hockey, and Calla misses him like crazy, but she'd never put any pressure on him to pick the closest team. If he's a Blizzard now, I have to believe it's for more reasons than one…

His eyes find mine first, and then his smile softens. His head tilts a bit as he stares at me for a moment before he's jostled by Jake, and then they're both walking toward our booth. My stomach flips in the best sort of way with every step he takes.

"Hey," he greets, saying the word to me first, his eyes twinkling with affection. I wouldn't be surprised if I'm wearing a matching expression while staring at him in return. *Heart eyes.* The guy has *heart eyes* for me, and it has my soul singing loudly for him.

Calla interrupts the moment we'd momentarily been sharing by asking, "Sean Spruce, do you want to update me on anything?' She pulls him into a hug, then she's reaching for Jake next. "Hi Jake, it's so nice to see you again."

Am I imagining things, or is Calla blushing a little as she gazes up at Jake? He is pretty to look at, but he's got nothing on Sean as far as I'm concerned. I swear I witness a twinkle in his eye as he meets her gaze, but I must be mistaken. *Surely. That's Sean's mom!*

"Brenda, Gram, Winter, this is my buddy Jake. Mom, I told Jake he could stay at the house until he gets his living arrangements situated. I hope that's okay."

Jake steps forward, offering me his hand to shake. "What he means to say is that I'm his best friend. The same friend who just switched teams to the *Blizzards,* so we can continue to play together."

He moves to Gram next, but he doesn't shake her hand; he lightly kisses the top, and I swear she swoons. It's hilarious. He tries it on Mom, but her brow goes up and she gives him her best 'professional doctor look' and he ends up shaking hers. I can't help but smirk at the show playing out before me. Jake shakes things up, and I'm going to enjoy every moment of him being around. He pulls Calla into another hug, keeping her tucked under his arm as they separate, and I don't miss how red her cheeks are at having his attention.

He leans in, whispering to her, "Hey, roomie. Thanks for letting me stay with you."

Calla is stunned at first, but then she's pinning her attention on her son as she tears up, asking, "Is he serious, Sean? It's true you've signed a contract with the Blizzards?"

He glances at me for a moment as if he's weighing my reaction before nodding and addressing the group. "I had to fly to New York suddenly when I learned I was about to be traded from the Pines. I'm sure you've seen the news by now; it's all over the place that the Pines were on the cusp of going bankrupt. They had to make some quick, expensive trades to stay afloat. I was one of them, and when my agent told me the Blizzards were interested in me, I jumped at the chance to be this close to home." He smiles at his mom's happiness, then turns his attention back on me. "Can we talk? Maybe go for a quick skate?"

"We're glad to have you so close to home again, honey," Mom says, with a quick, affectionate pat against his bicep. They're like bricks, I remember all too well from touching him and spending our night together. Yep, the man has arms that are brag-worthy.

"About time you got your head out of your rear and came to play for the home team, and you brought a new cute one with you, so I'll accept it." Gram nods her approval.

I roll my eyes and shake my head, watching as his lips fight from laughing at Gram's comments. "I could stretch my legs for a minute," I respond, trying to act like I'm not freaking out inside right now over this news. He'll be so much closer now, considering he used to be in New York, and I live and work in the opposite direction from Noel Falls. Now, we'll only be a few hours apart on a good weather day.

"Oh heavens, Winter, take more than a moment! And, you better lay one on the man in the middle of that skating rink before everyone else around here learns he's home for good." Gram shoots me a look, telling me she means business, and suddenly, I can't escape with Sean fast enough. I grab his hand, tugging him away from the booth as Mom and Calla laugh at something Jake says, but it's too low for me to hear.

"In a rush?" Sean asks as we practically jog to the ice skate rental booth. We both own our own skates, but neither of us is prepared.

"From Gram? One hundred percent yes. Have you been paying attention to the stuff she says?"

He chuckles, "I actually find her candor refreshing. Being around fake people for years will make you appreciate the real ones much more when you get to be around them."

We stop at the counter with a basket of thick socks for purchase and a metal foot measure thingy. "I'll take a size seven, and he'll have a thirteen, please," I say to the young girl working the skate rental booth. She's lucky she has a portable heater in there with her. I bet her toes aren't as cold as mine are.

"You remember my skate size?"

I shrug the question off, wondering if I'm showing my cards too soon. I take the last drink of my peppermint hot cocoa and toss the cup in the trash as Sean pays for our rental skates, then we're lacing up our skates together on the closest bench. He smells so good, like soap, fresh snow, and cologne all mixed into one. He leans over, pressing a kiss to the top of my head.

"What was that for?" I murmur, already feeling breathless as I stand.

He follows suit, grabbing my hand and lacing our gloved fingers together. "I didn't get to kiss you in the booth, and I missed you."

"You did?" I can't help but question as he leads me out on the ice. His hand holds mine tightly, offering me a little more balance. I like how he's always so thoughtful and helpful, even when I don't ask him to be.

"Of course I did. I couldn't stop thinking about you the entire time I was away from you. I wanted to text a dozen times, but made myself wait. I know how busy and worried you've been with the farm, and I didn't want to take away any more of your time and cause you more stress."

"Sean..." I trail off as we make a loop around the rink. I keep peaking under my lashes over at him, taking in his large frame. He seems normal-sized when he's on the ice with his teammates, but having him beside me like this reminds me just how big he really is. Six foot-four, broad shoulders, muscular, but not beefy. He's literally a walking dream man come true, but he acts like he doesn't have the slightest clue people see him in such a way.

"What? It's true, Winter. You seem to be all I think about these days, and I don't want it to change."

I stop skating, admitting, "I think of you all the time."

He turns toward me, grabbing my other hand so he holds both of them. "I planned to see if we could make things between us work despite the distance our jobs and homes put us at. But now," he grows quiet as he stares into my eyes. His gaze conveys so much, but I need to hear him actually say it out loud so I know we're on the same page.

"Now?"

He nods. "The moment I heard the Blizzards wanted me, I was ready to sign the contract. I had already wanted to be closer to home to be near my mom, which is why I've been spending so much time visiting, but then I saw you again. Things have changed for me, and I no longer only need to be close to watch out for my mom, but because I can't stand the thought of spending more time apart from you."

"I don't want to be away from you either," I quietly confess. This is turning into a conversation that should only be between him and me, and yet there are people everywhere. I keep catching their curious eyes flicking to us and then away, attempting to be nonchalant, but they're not fooling me. They want the tea and will share it with their friends in a heartbeat; it's just the way things go in Noel Falls.

His hand releases mine as he reaches up to cup my jaw. I lean into his touch, loving how sweet he is and how cherished he makes me feel all in the span of a moment. "I'd never ask you to give up your career, but then, when I researched what you do, I learned you can work remotely. I thought…" He trails off with a shrug.

"You're right, I do merchandise ordering for some department stores and marketing. I've been there long enough that I can pretty much work remotely if I wish, but the truth is, I've been unhappy with the company. I thought my vacation time would be enough, but then, when I got here and learned my father was hurt, and the farm needs me, it got me thinking, too. Throw in the fact that I almost couldn't pay my bills because my card information was cloned or whatever, and I started to think it was all a sign. I decided that maybe I should consider moving back home for a while."

"For a while? How long?"

I shrug. "Until I can get back on my feet and figure things out at least. Maybe find a new job, one I'll actually enjoy this time around."

"What if you didn't have to work? What if you could help with the farm and spend your free time doing whatever makes you happy?"

I laugh. "Yeah, dream come true. Where's my winning lottery ticket to make it happen?"

His finger gently rubs over my cheek as he says, "I want you to stay here, Winter. Only if it'll make you happy. But I don't want you living with your parents, I want you building your life with me instead."

"A life with you? What would that look like?"

He nods, a small smile tipping his lips, "Yes. Help me find a house that we can make into a home, or we can have one built, whatever would make you happier. Start your own business if you want to, or maybe start a family with me? Only if you're ready. I won't pressure you on anything. I just need you in my life. Now that I'm playing for the Blizzards, and we're close to your family, I can finally offer you what I've always wanted when it comes to you."

"Oh, Sean. You dumb, gorgeous, considerate hockey man. I would've followed you across the world with nothing in our pockets, if you'd have asked me to."

"I know, but you would've been miserable being so far away from here, and I never could've lived with myself if I made you unhappy. So what do you think? Will you stay here and finally be mine?"

"I can't believe you haven't figured it out by now."

His brow furrows, "What?"

"I've been yours from the moment you looked my way, and I always will be. I'm hopelessly in love with you. In fact, I'm pretty sure I've loved you from the first time you danced with me at the Jingle Bell Swing, and I'm just now realizing that's why it hurt so badly to think about you over the years we've been a part."

"I promise to spend the rest of our lives making them up to you. I'll always be the bell to your jingle. The berry to your holly. The tree to your ornament. The nog to your egg. The toe to your mistle-"

I interrupt with a laugh, "I'm going to hold you to that. Tinsel to my tangle."

He winks, "Exactly. And I hope you do. Winter to *my* wonderland." He says softly, leaning down until he's close enough that our noses nearly touch.

My arms move up around his neck, shimmying my body closer to his. He slides his hands around my waist, and then his lips are on mine, needing no mistletoe to tell us what to do. He holds me tightly in the middle of the skating rink and kisses me like I'm his only Christmas wish.

Like I'm his entire world.

I already know he's mine, and this Christmas, I'm getting everything I've asked for.

SAPPHIRE KNIGHT

Chapter Twenty-Four

SEAN

TWO WEEKS LATER...

"Is this the one?" I ask, glancing around at the open concept floor plan of the recently renovated home we're currently standing in. Winter told me it's her least favorite type of house setup, but the wall of windows with the view of the snowy mountains in the back of the property has left her a bit speechless. I don't think the open concept matters much anymore with a view like that, and I don't blame her.

"Do you like it?" She questions with a glance in my direction, but she doesn't need to. I will literally love anything that makes her happy. I want her to pick whatever house or land for us to build on that will have her wanting to spend the rest of her life with me, because that's the next step. My ultimate goal. She glances around, hands resting on her hips as she comments, "It's a lot of money. Nancy even said it's a bit over-priced."

"The only thing that matters to me is if you'll be here. Anything else is a bonus. If the floor plan is throwing you off, but you love everything else, then we'll remodel. We'll do whatever we need to so you're comfortable and happy in a home you love. I want to grow old with you, Winter. Everything else is just details we can figure out as we come to them."

She steps closer, her head tipped back so she can meet my gaze as I wrap my arms around her. "You're right. Sometimes I still feel the need to pinch myself, to make sure this is all real. That you're actually here and with me."

She's already got an understated promise ring on her finger that I put there a couple of weeks ago, right after I asked her to be my girlfriend in the middle of the park's ice rink. She's crazy if she thinks I'm not putting the biggest diamond I can afford on her next. I don't care if she's afraid to draw attention to it or not; I want everyone to know she's mine. I told her I'm going to propose, but I'm trying to wait at least a few months so her family doesn't think we're rushing things too quickly. While this is our relationship and her happiness is my ultimate goal, I still respect her family and want to cause the least amount of stress on Winter as possible. I explained my reasoning to her and I think she appreciates it more that I was open about everything, rather than her left believing I'm not ready to fully commit. Because I most certainly am.

If I could put her in my pocket and carry her around, I would. I'm that certain about us, and there's no way I'll be changing my mind. Ever.

"I don't want to be anywhere else but with you. One benefit of this place being move-in ready is that we'll get to start sharing a bed each night." Without worrying about ruffling our families' feathers or getting randomly snowed in at the cabin. That can't happen again until the season's over and I'm finally able to spend all my time with her like the needy man I've turned out to be. Capable, yes, however, I want to spend all my time with my woman, and when we're a part, it kinda feels like the end of the world if I'm being honest.

"And there's already a Christmas tree. Kind of ironic, since we got snowed in together all in the name of cutting a tree down." She gestures to the massive real spruce centered in front of the windows. It's undecorated aside from white twinkle lights. The rest of the place is bare, just a blank canvas for however my woman wants to decorate it, but putting a tree in the space was a nice touch. I know my Christmas crazy girlfriend will certainly appreciate having it here to admire, and also one less thing on her new to-do list will be checked off. "I say if the tree's here, then we're here," she shrugs, and I grin like a fool because she's so freaking cute.

"The tree and the mountains…" she trails off for a beat before continuing, "We could put some chairs right out there on the porch with one of those small gas fire tables so we could sit outside and take in the fresh air. Maybe make some smores," she smirks. She's already making plans, seeing us in the space, so it's a done deal. This is the house where we'll make all of our future important memories, and I can't wait for every single one.

"I like that suggestion, and also how there are thirty acres. Plenty of room for us to do what we want out here. Big shower, enough room for two."

"We could build a family cabin like my parents."

"Yes, that's a good idea, and also, stick a hot tub out back. You could wear a bikini, or nothing." I suggest trying to be nonchalant, but now I'm seeing us in every space here, too. "Maybe hang a little mistletoe around the place."

She stares for a moment longer and then finally nods, newfound excitement filling her gaze. "Okay, Sean. Let's do it. This is the one for us. And sign me up for the hot tub, mistletoe, and oversized shower."

"You got it, gumdrop. Let me tell Nancy to put in a low offer and see what the owners come back with."

"Isn't that considered rude?"

I shrug. "We're going to have to do a lot of remodeling to make this into what we want it to be, so I don't think so. Plus, they'll counter with an offer and we'll go back and forth, hopefully anyhow, if they're reasonable."

"And if they're not?"

"Then we'll keep looking until we find someplace that takes our breath away. I'm not rushing this with us. I plan to savor every moment I have with you, my love."

She squeezes me tightly, then steps out of my embrace, leaving me to speak to our realtor while she pokes around the living area and stops to stare out into the back of the property. It's a winter wonderland out there, so I can't blame her. One day, we'll be out there building snowmen and then again assembling a swing set. We'll spend our nights under the twinkling stars and warm in the hot tub when the crisp, cool evenings give us another excuse to spend time together. We'll roast marshmallows, grow a garden, and maybe even put a pool in. This will be the place we have our first fight as a couple, and this'll be the same place that I'll do anything I can to make sure she knows how much I love her and will do whatever I have to do to make sure we live this life together.

The house has been on the market for a little while, and Nancy says it's out of most people's price range around here, so I'm hoping the owners are motivated to sell. Either way, I meant what I said to Winter. I need all the time I can possibly get with her, and I'm not rushing anything. I want to make sure she's truly happy because now that we're together, I can no longer imagine my life without her at the center of it all.

"Nancy, please put in the lowest offer you think is reasonable. I don't want to offend the owners, but we'll have to do a lot of work to make it into what Winter wants. We love the windows, the property, and the fact that we can close and move in pretty much tomorrow."

"It is beautiful. It's a shame you both don't like how it's been updated already; it would save you a lot of time and hassle. But the wood everywhere is a little overpowering, and I'd be painting or something too."

"I agree. We're making this into our forever home, and since we aren't building it new, it'll need work. You still have that contractor hook-up you were bragging about a few months back when I talked to you about updating Mom's place?"

She nods, her short curly hair hairsprayed in place to the point it doesn't move at all. She's got on a bright purple suit, which would look ridiculous on anyone else, but with the bleached and feathered hairstyle, her oversized jewelry, and outgoing personality, it somehow suits her. "My nephew, yes, he's wonderful. I'll make sure and give you his information. I have a feeling the owners will accept your offer or close to it; they're ready to retire in Florida and not worry about this place anymore. They'll love the idea of it going to a new family, too."

We leave, hopeful, and our hearts racing with the next step we're taking together. This really is turning out to be the best Christmas I've had since my father passed away, and I have Winter to thank for it.

Nancy works her magic, and an hour later, we've negotiated until both parties are okay with the price, and I get to share the good news with my sweet woman. She's been patient with me through all the back-and-forth texting, and I'm glad to see it wasn't all for nothing.

"Hey, beautiful?" I shift until I'm facing Winter.

We've just had a late lunch and now we're sipping hot cocoa while snuggled close together, riding in a horse-drawn carriage. It's carrying us through Noelville's park, that's been lit up with tons of Christmas lights. It's still daytime, but not very bright out with the overcast clouds, so it's the perfect time to enjoy a daytime ride. There's fresh popcorn being popped, carols being played by violin, hot cocoa, coffee, and cider for sale, and a few other festive things in the park. It's not as busy as the Noel Falls community festival was, but it's still neat being out here.

Winter shivers, and I quickly tuck more of the fleece blanket around her. The driver had given it to us when we first climbed in to help keep us warm. "Yes?"

"I've got good news. Nancy just texted me that the owners have accepted our last offer. The house is ours, and when we're done here, we can head over to her office to read through the paperwork. I asked her to send everything to my lawyer already so he can review it for us from a legal standpoint. I hope you're ready for this."

"I'm more than ready. I'm so excited right now I could run across the park to your truck." She laughs, and I smile in return. I know exactly how she feels because I'm the same way right now.

"You're it for me. I told you that before, but I mean it. I am so hopelessly in love with you. I can't wait to buy this house with you. Next, we get married, and then finally, we spend our lives together, growing old and gray. This is the happiest I can ever remember being, and it's all because of you." I confess.

A tear escapes, leaving a wet trail down her cheek as she softly smiles. It's sweet and full of so much emotion. She's stunning like this, absolutely beautiful, and she's all mine to love and hold, to cherish and protect.

I can't wait. I lean in, dipping a bit until my lips press to hers. My kiss is soft and slow, as I attempt to convey just how much she means to me. When we pull away, I gently rest my forehead against hers and tuck a few strands of her hair behind her ear.

"I love you, Sean, so much. I'm ready to spend my forever with you, and I can't imagine being anywhere else than in your arms each night when I fall asleep. You already know my answer, so when the time comes, I will be ready and waiting to walk down that aisle with you. Whether it's in a grocery store, hand in hand, so we can cook dinner together, or if it's to a preacher, so he can promise us to each other in front of God and our families, you can count on me."

And then they lived happily ever after, driving each other crazy with home remodels, kids, and dogs that bark way too much. But most of all, they lived their lives with love and warmth, patience and kindness, support and tenderness, and in the end, they found a love together like no other.

True love.

THANK YOU

Thank you for reading my sweet, feel-good romance about Sean and Winter! I hope you enjoyed *Snowed in with My Pucking Ex* and will consider leaving a positive review. Every bit helps, and spreading the word about books and authors you love is its own type of special magic to us. In case no one has told you, you are appreciated. Your kindness and cheer during the season are what make the world so great this time of year.

Merry Christmas, I hope you have the happiest of holidays!

Sending big hugs,

-Sapphire

SAPPHIRE KNIGHT

About the Author

Sapphire Knight is a Wall Street Journal, USA Today, and Amazon International Bestselling Author. Her books all reflect what she loves to read herself. She's a Texas girl at heart who's crazy about football and has always possessed a passion for writing. She originally studied psychology and feels that it's added to her drive for writing diverse characters.

Sapphire is the proud mom of two handsome boys and loves to donate to help animals. When she's not busy in her writing cave, she's playing with her three Doberman Pinschers.

www.authorsapphireknight.com

And also find her on Bookbub!

OTHER BOOKS BY SAPPHIRE KNIGHT

Oath Keepers MC Series

Exposed (2nd chance, very spicy)

Relinquish

Forsaken Control (MMF, taboo)

Friction (brother's best friend)

Sweet Surrender –

free short story in my newsletter

Ten Minutes (size difference)

Oath Keepers MC Hybrid Series

Princess (obsessive & possessive)

Love and Obey –

free short story in my newsletter

Daydream (one night stand)

Baby (MMF, unhinged)

Chevelle (alpha vs. alpha)

Cherry (reverse age gap, family drama)

Heathen (kidnapping/Stockholm)

Hollywood (age gap, single parent)

Death Dealer (jailbreak, unhinged MFC & dom MMC)

Russkaya Mafiya Series

Secrets (college romance)

Corrupted (age gap romance)

Corrupted Counterparts –

free short story in my newsletter

Unwanted Sacrifices (2nd chance, teddy bear mmc)

Undercover Intentions (trafficking, Stockholm)

Dirty Down South Series

Freight Train (sweet & spicy football romance)

3 Times the Heat (rancher & feisty MFC romance)

Bliss (cowboy stripper turned coach)

Falling for the Quarterback SPIN-OFF (JJ, reverse age gap, later in life football romance)

The Vendetti Famiglia (dark mafia romance, forced prox, cnc, breeding, billionaire)

SAPPHIRE KNIGHT

The Vendetti Empire (age gap, arranged marriage, cnc)

The Vendetti Queen

The Vendetti Seven (trafficking, forced breeding)

The Vendetti Coward (drug addiction, surprise baby, nanny)

The Vendetti Daddy (age gap, asphyxiation, dominant, controlling)

The Vendetti Devil (birth control tampering, arranged marriage)

The Vendetti Soldier (mmfm, cnc, arranged marriage, squirting)

The Vendetti Casanova (Coming Soon)

Harvard Academy Elite (light bully reverse harem romance)

Little White Lies (quads, mental health rep, deception)

Ugly Dark Truth

RBBBMC TX - Patched over to OKMC

Opposites Attract/Bastard Biker (bargaining, age gap, steamy)

Dirty Biker (undercover cop, snowed in, one bed)

Toxic Biker (brother's best friend, dominant)

Protective Biker (size difference, deaf MFC, forced fit)

Kings of Carnage MC Series (small town, one-percenter)

Bash (woman on the run, dirty talker)

Sterling (brother's best friend, mask play, forbidden)

Tyrant (cult, hitchhiker, single mom)

The Chicago Crew (mafia, stalking, deception)

Gangster (spicy, dark themes, stalker)

Mad Max (jealous, blood play, dark romance, villain)

Kings of Anarchy MC – Central TX (breeding romance, cowboys, bikers)

Property of Madman (heavy breeding, reverse age gap, morally gray)

Property of Death (coming soon)

VII Knights MC (loosely based on Sleeping Beauty)

Hunter (primal play, age gap, billionaire)

Brotherhood of Darkness (secret society romance, MFM, mask play, stalking, obsessive, possessive, jealous, gun play, unhinged mmc)

(Co-Author Hilary Storm)

Order of Obsession

Vow of Vengeance

Saints Outlaws MC – Austin, TX

Reaper's Revenge (vampire, fated mates, spicy, later in life, strong mfc, protective MMC romance)

Extras

The Main Event –

free short story previously published in my newsletter

Tease – (Short Story Collection, MMF, pregnancy, holiday, fighting, family drama, spicy)

Viking –

free short story previously posted in my newsletter

Dirty Down South Collection

Naughty Good Girl (Father's best friend romance, age gap, spanking, public sexual punishment, holiday, billionaire, forced proximity, traded for debt)

Carnal Addiction (standalone Russian mafia, loan shark, reverse age gap, single father, forced proximity, kidnapping, Stockholm syndrome, holidays, spicy, mental health rep)

Unexpected Forfeit (MMA romance, spicy, sweet but protective hero, beach read, strong mfc, fighting)

Snowed in with My Pucking Ex (Hockey holiday standalone, sweet but steamy, teddy bear hero, he falls first, feisty mfc)

ACKNOWLEDGMENTS

My Boys—You're my whole world. I love you with every beat of my heart, and I will forever. Thank you for being just as Christmas crazy as your mom.

My Dogs—My favorite non-humans in the entire world! I love them so much it's crazy.

Motorcycles, Mobsters, and Mayhem Author Event. It's changed my life, and I love hosting this themed event to bring so many wonderful people together. I hope I will see you at the next one!

Robbie— Your kind words and continued support have helped motivate me to continue this one. I'm so happy you are loving this softer side of my books, too. Thank you!

My Readers—I love you. You make my life possible, so thank you. I can't wait to meet many of you this year and in the future. To those of you who leave me the awesome spoiler-free reviews, you motivate me to keep writing. For that, I'll forever be grateful, as this is my passion in life.

And as always, ADOPT DON'T SHOP! Save a life today and adopt from a rescue or your local animal shelter.

Made in the USA
Coppell, TX
04 March 2026

73186333R00152